The Art
of Villainy

SanTaro DeBose

BOOKS BY SANTARO DEBOSE

The Art of Villainy

Table of Contents

1. Dances and Disasters   7
2. Dawn and Dilemmas   17
3. The #1 Rule   27
4. The Forces of the Universe   39
5. The Art of Villainy   53
6. The Queen   69
7. Franklin   77
8. Hell   99
9. Avenger   111
10. Plots and Plans   123
11. The Governor's Ball   131
12. The Funeral   151
13. Piracy   163
14. Making History   175

15. The Spectator   181

16. The First Universal Bank   189

17. Reloading   199

18. Choices   205

19. The Quasar   221

20. Apostate   227

21. Liberation   235

22. Operation Valiant   249

23. Mediation   257

24. Stellar Run   261

25. War and Peace   275

26. Utopia   287

27. Uncharted Space   307

28. The Many Star Systems   321

1. Dances and Disasters
"And people think I'm crazy, right?"

The Union rules everything within the Asteroid Belt. The only way to achieve anything, to become anyone of value in society, is through the Union. The mega rich - cinema stars, athletes, broadcasters, influencers and politicians – reside on lavish Mars. Everyone else is left to survive on a downtrodden Earth.

It is late in Meridian, a small city in the northwest hemisphere of Earth. Cantinas and clubs are the only establishments open at this hour. Sidewalks buzzing with hardworking Union citizens during the day are now filled with weekenders; a generation of youth lost between Union control and rebellion. With each passing day, they inch closer towards allegiance or anarchy.

Tonight, the wayward youngsters are dressed in bright neon colors and covered in face paint. Their only goal is to drink until they vomit and dance until their legs turn to mush. Meridian is a party mecca.

Samuel Henry Bragg has recently deserted the Union's military, the Space Force.

He wanders the crowded sidewalks aimlessly, taking gulps from a pint of synthetic alcohol. The collar of his navy-blue jacket is flipped up, concealing his face from the sides. A laser pistol is holstered against his side. The fear of being apprehended has worn Bragg down. He seeks reprieve from anxiety at the bottom of the flimsy plastic bottle.

Tall, foreign buildings line both sides of the street. The city is covered with a comfortable filth. Bragg feels every bit the excursionist. The population seems to have tripled since his last visit, a godsend for someone ensconced. Bragg hides in plain sight among hundreds of pedestrians.

The alcohol begins to blur his vision. His legs become noodles as he struggles to maintain balance. Taking a moment to regain his bearings, Bragg leans against a chain link fence next to the sidewalk. The euphoric effect of his beverage is wearing off, handing his body over to dizziness and nausea.

Buried beneath Bragg's booze-fueled haze lie suppressed memories. If he stays sober too long, Bragg is certain the consequences of his past actions will come flooding back into his life.

As his vision clears, fuzzy moving shapes morph into partiers passing Bragg by. They all ignore him as if he were discarded garbage. Each partier has his or her eyes glued to their

WristTop: a wristband with a six-inch computer screen that no one ever takes off. Bragg goes on watching them, amazed they don't collide with each other. He imagines where each person is going and who they are going to meet. This helps combat his loneliness.

Mixed in with the crowd of partiers lies a seedier sort. Men and women with a different style, which consists of tattoos and baggy clothing. Most are wearing solid colors and have poorly concealed weapons. Some throw up hand signs, subtle but noticeable to Bragg, even in his current state.

Bragg resumes his drunken stroll. Hover traffic - vehicles with round, smooth frames - blows past him, whipping his open jacket with violent gusts. To escape the wind, he staggers down steps that descend from the sidewalk, toward the basement of an inconspicuous building.

At the foot of the steps lies an opaque glass door. A pink neon sign above it reads *"THE OFFICE, gentlemen's club."* The music inside is so vibrant, Bragg can feel the bass rumbling beneath his feet. A doorman stands guard. He wears shades and a black shirt. His head is bald and his expression is unfriendly.

Bragg meanders over. Without saying a word, the man points to a black sign with gold lettering:

20 credits – Gentlemen
FREE – Ladies

Bragg pulls up his left jacket sleeve and holds out his WristTop. The doorman scans away the entry credits with a tablet, then points at the laser pistol on Bragg's hip.

"That has to stay with me." The doorman speaks in a faux-authoritative tone.

Bragg pauses a moment before unbuckling his holster belt and untying the strap around his right thigh. *If the doorman is confiscating weapons, then everyone inside should be unarmed.* Bragg shoves the laser pistol and holster into the doorman's arms.

The doorman frowns at first, then steps aside and opens the opaque door behind him.

The entrance opens to a dinky shotgun cellar, bustling with activity. A bar comprises the entire left side of the risqué hideaway. Shelves of liquor line the wall behind it from the floor to the ceiling, back lit with neon colors. Topless females giggle and pour drinks for gawking men who line the barstools.

There is a stage along the wall opposite the bar. Six poles are illuminated with spotlights across the stage, showcasing male and female dancers. A DJ booth sits in the backdrop.

Bragg's nostrils are assaulted with the scent of sweat and lust. Soft blue light sticks to everything. Electronic cigarette vapor is suspended in the air. Techno hip hop blares, making his ears ring.

Eight or so round tables are spread out between the bar and stage, each with its own pole on top. Bragg strolls in and finds a seat at a table in the back. From the secluded corner, Bragg has clear sight of the entire club. *There appears to be only one way in and out.*

A man sits at a separate table, across from Bragg. He has a full head of blonde hair and a beer belly. The man smiles as a female wearing a red bikini dances atop his table. He raises his WristTop towards a nearby kiosk, tipping credits and yelling with excitement. Bragg wishes he was having that much fun.

When the DJ changes the music, a door behind the bar flies open. More dancers erupt into the club.

Bragg's gaze shifts and finds a dancer with lengthy purple pigtails sashaying toward his table. Lipstick matching her hair has been meticulously applied to her full lips, which are parted into a seductive smirk. She is so bewitching it startles Bragg.

A black one-piece barely covers the dancer's slim, muscular frame. Her alluring breasts are exposed with only purple skull pasties covering her nipples.

The dancer locks eyes with Bragg. Sharp purple pupils hide behind her long eyelashes. Her look is intoxicating, inviting him to take a tour of her damaged past.

The neon lights give the dancer an exotic glow. She climbs up onto Bragg's table and stands over him authoritatively, with both hands on her hips. Her black six-inch heels have purple bottoms.

The dancer squats, winking at Bragg before gracefully twirling around the pole and syncing with the beat of the music. She lip syncs the song's words as she gyrates her hips. With agility, she climbs the pole higher and locks her thighs, pigtails flailing as she hangs upside down. Bragg forgets there are others in the club.

When the song ends, the dancer steps off the table and sits sideways across Bragg's lap. He squeezes her gently. Unintentionally. Her body is the perfect blend of firmness and softness.

The dancer pulls an e-cigarette from her hair and places it between her lips. She puts an arm around Bragg's neck, rubbing the backside of his faded haircut. Her palm is like a billion tiny pillows on his skin. Peach perfume gives her a pleasant fragrance.

She rubs beneath Bragg's jacket, running her fingers against his chest. His body melts at her touch. She continues to puff the cigarette, leaving a faint lipstick stain on the aluminum cartridge.

When the DJ starts another song, the dancer hands Bragg the e-cigarette.

He holds it flimsy between his fingers before taking a drag. The vapor is like inhaling flames as it passes his throat and Bragg coughs harshly. Tears swell his eyes.

Idiot! You've never smoked e-cigs.

The dancer climbs back onto the table, giggling at him, "Having trouble?"

Her voice is dominant with a unique feminine charm. Bragg doubts anyone has ever denied her anything.

The sudden zapping sounds of laser rounds echo throughout the club. The noise sends a jolt through Bragg's spine.

A half-dozen orange-dressed men come through the entrance. Each is armed with a military grade rifle.

They found me.

"Not again," the dancer whispers, visibly shaken.

Bragg grabs the dancer's forearms and pulls her off the tabletop. He flips the table on its side, breaking the pole on top and sheltering her behind it. The intruders sporadically fire rounds into the ceiling, causing the club patrons to panic and scurry around.

The beer-bellied man knocks over tables and shoves dancers to the floor as he rushes for the bar. Just before he reaches the stools, one of the intruders fires a laser round into his back. His blubbery body drops to the floor like an ancient walrus.

The heartless murder sends the club into a frenzy. People trample each other, desperate to escape the madness. The intruders spread through the club, continuing to kill without any sense of regard.

Bragg reaches for the pistol on his hip, grasping only air. *Great job, doorman.* His vision is still hazy from the alcohol but his mind is racing. Through the crowd, he notices two of the intruders approaching with rifles at the ready.

"Is there another exit?" Bragg asks the dancer.

"Behind . . . hind . . . the bar, through the dressing room . . ." she answers, her voice barely audible.

Bragg spots the dressing room door. He grabs the dancer and cradle-carries her as he zigs and zags his way through the buzzing crowd, bumping into the jostling bodies.

Pshhwoom! Pshhwoom! Bright red laser rounds whiz past, so close Bragg can feel their heat. The bar is five or so feet away.

Just a little farther.

Bragg dives over the bar top, using it as cover. The dancer falls out of his arms as he hits the floor. Bottles on the shelf above are destroyed from the rounds, raining shards on Bragg.

Through squinted eyes, Bragg can see the dancer ahead of him bear-crawling toward the dressing room. He crawls after her. Scrapes form on his hands from pieces of broken glass.

I may not survive this.

Bragg and the dancer make it through the dressing room door. They stand up and continue down a narrow row of metal lockers.

The dancer's heels produce pattering *clicks* on the tile floor. "This way!" she urges, turning left at the end of the row.

They arrive at an emergency exit, running through the door without stopping. Cool night air strikes Bragg as he emerges into the alley behind the club. The path is dark and unpleasant, reeking from dumpsters overflowing with trash. Bragg struggles to catch his breath, looking around for a place to keep fleeing.

"We have to get out of here," the dancer urges.

"We should split up. I think they are after me," Bragg confesses.

"They are after everybody. Come on! I've got a hoverbike stashed away."

Bragg still considers parting ways with the dancer, but he knows the chaos inside will surely draw the attention of Enforcers. Bragg decides he does not want to be wandering around when they arrive.

A few yards down the alley, they come to a large object that's covered by a thin tan sheet. The dancer rips the sheet off, revealing a hoverbike. It has a narrow, octahedron-shaped metal frame that is painted grey with *HONDA* sprawled down the side in bold red letters. A leather seat covers the top, sloping upward toward the end to serve as a backrest for a passenger. The stubby handlebars bow backward and project a digital display from the center.

"Why do you keep your bike behind the club?" Bragg asks.

"For situations like this. And people think I'm crazy, right?"

The dancer straddles the bike. Propulsion engines beneath the frame roar to life, producing a blue light and levitating it from the ground. She takes a helmet from a compartment in the center and places it on her head.

Bragg removes his jacket and holds it out for the dancer.

"Thank you," the dancer says, her voice muffled through the helmet. She places her arms through the extended jacket sleeves. "I'm Dawn, by the way."

"I'm Bragg," he replies, as he climbs onto the back of the bike.

-----

2. Dawn and Dilemmas
"Living on Mars is only glamorous for Martians."

Dawn Kheela squeezes the handle grips so tightly they feel attached to her hands. The hoverbike beneath her tears through the streets of Meridian, darting in and out of the sparse traffic.

Bragg is riding behind Dawn with a one-armed grip around her waist. His skin is mocha. His dark hair is neat, fading from thick at the top to a mere shadow around his ears. His face is clean shaven and his jaw is square.

Oncoming night air bombards Dawn. She's wearing Bragg's open jacket and it flaps beneath her arms. Her fingers are icicles and her body is shivering.

After tonight's events, Dawn questions if she is still alive or a spirit going through the motions. The near-death experience back at The Office has forced a revelation upon her; she has wasted her life. Dancing during sleeping hours, partying during waking hours, drinking and taking narcotics nonstop. Countless squandered years.

I'm more than a working girl.

"So, what happened back there?" Bragg asks, as the bike slows down.

His deadpan voice startles her. "What?"

"Back at the club?"

"The Asteroids happened. Again."

"Who are the Asteroids?"

"They are some gang from Comet City, trying to move in on the Villains' turf." Dawn continues maneuvering the hoverbike.

"And who are the Villains?" asks Bragg.

Who is this guy? A tourist?

"Where are you from?"

"Somewhere else."

"Who did you think the Asteroids were? Who is after you?"

"Well… it's a long story . . ."

Dawn is too consumed by her situation to press Bragg any further. She returns to her own problems. "This is the third time the Asteroids have attacked. I'm never going back to The Office."

The words are satisfying as they leave her lips, but the reality is Dawn cannot afford to be without work. She is only a few thousand credits away from leaving Earth behind.

Dawn accelerates the hoverbike up an on-ramp, merging onto the highway above. Hover cars honk their horns as she slips ahead of the oncoming traffic, cutting several people off.

Yellow and red Enforcer lights flicker to life in the bike's mirrors. A droning siren cries through the air, causing the traffic ahead to pull to the side of the street. A voice blares through a speaker behind them. "PULL OVER NOW, OR WE WILL TAKE ACTION."

"We can't stop. They will arrest me," Bragg mumbles behind her. "We can't stop. We can't stop!"

Only look out for yourself.

While they had been in her life only briefly, Dawn's parents managed to instill that lesson. The simple advice has served her well.

However, an uncharacteristic sense of debt now clouds her judgement. Dawn doubts she would have escaped the massacre back at the club without aid from Bragg and begins to ponder her options. No fan of Enforcers herself, she has evaded their pursuit enough to feel confident about her odds.

Dawn hits the accelerator, honoring the mysterious stranger's request. As they enter the business district of Meridian, towering buildings surround the four-lane highway.

The squad car swerves to the left of the hoverbike, pulling up even with Dawn and matching speed. The squad car is dark with tinted windows. It has a bulky body with guard rails on the front and rear. *ENFORCERS* is spelled out across the doors of the sedan in bold white letters. Its belly thrusters growl in an unnerving way.

The highway tapers down to two lanes as they exit the business district. Dawn looks ahead a few hundred feet as cars and trucks float through a narrow intersection. The traffic light hanging above changes from green to yellow. She holds the accelerator down, inching the bike ahead of the Enforcers.

An automated semi-truck crossing through the intersection brakes hard, desperately trying to avoid Dawn's oncoming hoverbike. The Enforcer squad car pulls off and forfeits the impromptu game of chicken. As the traffic light turns red, Dawn's body tightens. She tries to draw a breath but can't.

Her hoverbike squeaks through the intersection and barely avoids the front of the semi-truck. There is a booming crash behind them followed by the howling screams of pedestrians. In the bike's mirrors, Dawn can see the semi and other traffic smashed together into a metallic heap. The Enforcer squad car is stuck on the other side of the pile-up accident and cut off from the pursuit.

Dawn slows the bike.

"Someone could be hurt," Bragg says, seemingly bothered.

"Want to go check, Mr. Fugitive?" Dawn replies, and keeps on driving.

The road outside downtown Meridian is dystopian. Streetlights are busted, with glass scattered below them like confetti. Homeless individuals are camped out in various places along the sidewalk, cocooned in blankets. Disabled vehicles line the curbs.

They reach Dawn's apartment. It's the top right unit of a rundown, two-story quadplex. She uses her fingers to dig a stashed key out of her hair, but then notices the doorknob is dangling from its place. The red door swings open with a slight nudge, revealing the pitch-black interior.

There is no sound. Dawn stumbles backwards. Her skin crawls with trepidation that someone is inside, going through her belongings or waiting to attack.

Bragg steps in front of Dawn and activates the flashlight on his WristTop. His tall, bulky body feels like a shield. The muscles on his back bulge through his white undershirt. The peaks of his shoulders are like mountain tops to Dawn.

With Bragg standing as a barrier between her and whatever lurks inside the apartment, Dawn begins to regain her composure.

Bragg moves inside, full stride and fearless.

Dawn waits a few moments and then follows.

She flicks the light switch on the wall, illuminating the seven-hundred-square-foot apartment. Her black leather couch and love seat are overturned just past the doorway. The cushions are cut open, their cotton insides sprawled all over the beige carpet. Missing dust marks the spots where her television and other valuables once sat. Dawn looks left towards the open kitchen. All the dark green cabinet doors are ajar and the shelves lie bare.

Oh, no.

Dawn hurries into the kitchen and rips open the flimsy cupboard underneath her sink. Her hidden safe is hacked open and an empty red can of *Best Selection* coffee sits inside. Her hard drive of credits and forged passport are gone.

"Damn it!" she yells.

Dawn throws the red can against the white kitchen wall. It hits with a bang before clattering around on the grey tile floor. She lets out another yell before smacking herself backward against the wall, sliding downward.

Sitting on the floor, knees clasped to her chest, Dawn stares at the coffee can now lying across from her. She feels just as empty.

I'll never get off this planet.

Bragg limps into the kitchen. His white undershirt is stained and dirty from the night's commotion. Dawn glares up at him, picking up on the dazed look in his eyes. He loses his balance, falling against the kitchen sink, but quickly pushes himself back up as if nothing happened.

"No one is here now," he mumbles.

Dawn gets up from the kitchen floor and walks over to look at him. His right thigh is partly burned. His dark pant leg is drenched in blood.

"You've been shot! Can't you feel it? We need to stop the bleeding."

He declines. "It won't matter much longer. I'll leave now." Bragg takes a few staggering steps toward the door.

The closer he gets, the bigger the knot in Dawn's stomach gets. After being shot at and burglarized, the last thing Dawn wants is to be left alone.

"I'm still wearing your jacket, you know." Dawn places her voice in a seductive octave.

Men listen better that way.

Bragg stands up taller and grabs at his chest, feeling for the jacket as if he doesn't believe her.

"I'll give it back . . . in the morning," she says. "The least I can do is let you crash on what's left of the couch. Enforcers are everywhere."

After a brief back and forth, Bragg reluctantly agrees to stay. Together they flip the leather couch right side over. Bragg sits down on it, pressing his hands into the cushions to test the softness.

Dawn enters the only bedroom. It has also been trashed. Blue sheets from her twin-size bed are on the floor. Her mattress is carved and gutted, the half-ounce of meteor dust she stashed inside is pilfered. The dresser drawers are open and rummaged. Dawn feels violated and without privacy.

She walks into the closet and finds her jewelry and purses missing.

At least they left my clothes.

Dawn removes Bragg's jacket and her stage outfit, replacing them with a baggy black t-shirt that drapes to her mid-thigh. She retrieves sheets and the first aid kit from the top of the closet.

In the living room, she finds Bragg sitting hunched over on the couch. She kneels down next to him, taking his calloused hand into hers. Grey eyes peek out from his drooped eyelids. They convey the pain he is in.

That pain is not just from the wound.

Although Dawn finds Bragg handsome, she can tell he is a bit younger than her. She rips his pant leg to expose the red, fleshy burn. Removing burn cream and gauze from the kit, Dawn begins to render aid. "Why are the Enforcers after you?" she asks, as she works.

Bragg sits in silence for a few moments, as if Dawn had said nothing at all. Finally he blurts out an answer: "I deserted the Space Force."

A chill comes across Dawn's body.

"Why would you leave the Space Force?" Dawn exclaims. "You get to live on Mars. Never worrying about credits or food."

"Living on Mars is only glamorous for Martians," Bragg replies.

Dawn sits back and looks at him. "Desertion is punishable by death. And so is harboring a deserter."

Bragg remains silent and allows her to go on wrapping his leg in gauze.

Although it makes Dawn uneasy, she chooses not to make an issue of Bragg's dilemma.

In fact, he may be the solution to my problem. Who better to get you off a planet than someone from space?

Dawn finishes wrapping his leg. "I think this should be good. It's no rehab chamber, but it is better than nothing."

"I should leave. Every second I'm here puts you in danger."

"Every second you're not here, I'm in danger. Look at my apartment."

This makes even the stoic Bragg grin. Dawn also smiles. Levity offers a brief break from the avalanche of trouble that life has dealt them both.

"I just . . ."

"It's settled," Dawn interrupts. "Get some rest. We will talk about what to do next tomorrow."

She gets up from beside the couch and heads to her bedroom. Her mind is already hard at work devising a way to get what she needs from Bragg.

-----

3. The #1 Rule
"There is a lot the Union hides from citizens."

A noisy bang jerks Bragg from deep slumber. He springs to his feet, disoriented, reaching down towards his hip. With no weapon, he scans the room in a panic.

All he sees is Dawn, standing in the kitchen of her apartment. Her purple hair is pulled into a high ponytail and her face is bare of makeup.

"I accidentally dropped a pan," Dawn says, with an annoyed look.

Sweat has moistened Bragg's undershirt – a souvenir of his nightmare. He continues to watch Dawn carefully. "Sorry. I just have this thing about being woken up."

"After last night, anyone would be jumpy."

Bragg realizes his memory from last night is foggy and missing chunks of time. His head feels like a cracked egg. The sour taste of synthetic alcohol stains his mouth. He plops back down onto the couch, holding his throbbing skull. His right thigh is on fire and wrapped in heavy gauze. His palms have tiny, burning cuts.

"I made breakfast from what my burglar left in the fridge." Dawn offers.

The kitchen is efficient. A stainless-steel refrigerator sits in the corner, next to the matching stove and oven. Bragg limps to the compact dining table and takes a seat. There's already a cold glass of ale waiting for him.

Dawn brings a skillet over from the stove and serves the steaming food onto plates. It's grilled eel and cheese.

Without hesitation Bragg grabs a fork and digs in, shoveling the food into his mouth. The normally bland eel is rich with seasoning and flavor. The ale is cold enough to sting his teeth as he gulps it down.

Not bad for Earth food.

Dawn sits across the table from him, barely picking at her plate as she watches Bragg.

He starts to notice that his manners have been lacking. "I'm sorry. I . . ." he starts.

"I'm glad you like it," Dawn says, smirking. She takes a few bites from her food but stops, as if she is displeased with her own cooking, and changes the subject. "Who is 'Trenton'?"

Trenton is dead.

Bragg finds himself suddenly fighting back tears. He wipes his dry cheeks, just in case, and looks Dawn in the eye. "How do you know that name?"

"You were saying it in your sleep." Her gaze is unrelenting.

Bragg knows nothing will satisfy her but a straight answer, and begins a story he'd rather not tell. "Trenton was my wingman in the 41st squadron. We were sent on a mission to bomb what we believed to be galactic terrorists on Earth."

He pauses. Dawn has not moved an inch since he started. It's as though she is frozen in time, refusing to budge until he finishes.

"During the mission, Trenton's fighter was shot down." Another pause; this one involuntary. A soft sob overtakes his speech. "I . . . couldn't save him."

Bragg closes his eyes.

My best friend.

The image of Trenton's fighter exploding into a million pieces is stuck on the inside of his eyelids.

"Eventually, I learned the terrorists could not be located. So, undisclosed to us, our mission was to bomb the city where their innocent families lived. They were only defending themselves . . ."

Women, children . . . they were just trying to stop us . . .

With his tale concluded, Bragg sits silently across from Dawn. He is damp faced and exposed. He has no clue why he just bared his innermost secrets to her, but in doing so he finds satisfaction. His only fear is how the beautiful dancer will judge him.

I have innocent blood on my hands.

Dawn reaches across the table and takes Bragg's hand compassionately, like an elder trying to console a mourning child. "You were right to leave."

Bragg feels, even if only for a moment, that Dawn understands what he is going through.

For a short time, they return to eating. Bragg glances at Dawn, attempting to be subtle. His heartbeat increases and butterflies fill his stomach. Even without makeup, her beauty is unrivaled.

"I was saving credits to be smuggled to Mars." Dawn interrupts the silence without looking up from her plate. "I always thought that was the answer. Is Mars really as horrible as you make it seem?"

"Mars is no oasis," Bragg replies. "Those born on Earth are treated like dirt."

"It must be better than here. There is nowhere in the solar system outside Union reach."

"Jupiter's moon, Europa." Bragg takes a few more bites of food, "It is allegedly home to enlightened beings."

"Life on Europa is a myth. Stories told to juveniles. It's inhabitable. You mean the Union believes someone lives there? Why would they hide that from citizens?"

"There is a lot the Union hides from citizens."

"Then forget Mars! You're a pilot. Let's just go to Europa ourselves."

"My fighter is not suited for such a long journey," Bragg explains.

Dawn looks down at her plate of food, disappointment sprawled across her face.

Bragg scrambles to find a way to comfort her. He has no idea why, but he would do anything to make her happy. "A larger ship could make the trip. And I know an Artificial Intelligence that . . ."

There is a loud and authoritative knock on the apartment door. *"Enforcers!* Dawn Kheela, open up. You're under arrest for eluding pursuit!"

Bragg and Dawn exchange panicked looks.

Immediately the Enforcers start to force their way in. The poorly repaired lock begins to loosen from the doorknob.

Dawn grabs Bragg's arm and yanks him halfway out of his seat. "You have to hide!" She pulls him into the tiny bathroom, then snatches open the cabinet beneath the sink. Dawn flips a switch, which causes the toilet to slide forward, revealing a hidden trapdoor.

Dawn raises the trapdoor. "Get in. Don't make a sound."

He does as instructed and shuts himself in. The space is cramped. His arms are pressed against his chest by the toilet's plumbing. His body is stuck in an awkward half squat.

Why does she have this hiding place?

Bragg listens for activity in the apartment above. He hears the Enforcers break down the door and storm inside. There is a round of commotion before Bragg hears their muffled voices.

"Where is he? Where is Commander Samuel Bragg?"

"I don't know who that is," Dawn insists.

"Impossible. He was with you last night. One more chance: Where is he?"

"Sarge! We found a jacket. It's his size," another Enforcer announces. "And the table is set for two. Food is still warm."

"Where is he?" shouts the Enforcer.

"Get . . . fucked," Dawn answers.

"Take her away."

The Enforcers begin tossing things around in the apartment. Bragg can hear crashes and shattering glass. There are creaking footsteps in the bathroom above. Anxiety oozes through Bragg as he hides, attempting to mask his breathing. The harder he tries to be quiet, the more of himself he hears.

Frustration overwhelms Bragg. He wants to do something, anything to save Dawn from the Enforcers.

They arrested her because of me.

Outgunned and outnumbered, Bragg knows he stands little chance.

But a squad man never gives up.

After waiting for what feels like days, Bragg finally hears nothing but silence in the apartment. He tries to push the trapdoor open, however the toilet above is blocking his escape.

"There has to be . . ."

His hand brushes a switch that slides the toilet forward and opens the trapdoor. Bragg emerges from hiding.

He finds himself alone in the aftermath. The place is even more disheveled than before. The walls have been smashed open to the point of exposing wooden beams. In the kitchen, Bragg finds Dawn's keys protruding from a pile of drywall on the floor.

Bragg ventures outside and finds the hoverbike still parked by the curb. He takes the handle grips and starts the ignition.

He rides the bike through Meridian until he reaches city limits. The busy metro highway turns into a two-lane road, surrounded by dusty desert plains. The sun cooks Bragg as he rides. His burnt right thigh plagues him with sharp pain. Determination alone drives him on. That, and thinking about Dawn.

Bragg has never had a romantic partner. Bullied in secondary school, he threw himself into studies and athletics. In the Space Force, companionship took lower priority to survival. However, something about Dawn captivates him and he finds himself constantly imagining a relationship with the irresistible entertainer.

As the sun sets over the horizon, Bragg reaches his destination. He stands on the edge of a vast ravine looking down at his VERON Mark IX fighter, resting on the bottom of a deep gorge.

The Mark IX has a broad, flat nose. Cylinder engines hug both sides of the fuselage, with short wings extending out from them. The cockpit sits atop the middle of the craft and is divided into two compartments: the pilot area in the front and space for a navigator behind. A rudder stands tall in the rear. Its light grey paint is accented by navy on the nose.

Manning the fighter again is tough for Bragg. The controls have not been touched since he flew for the Space Force.

There is no other choice.

Despite every reason, Dawn chose not to betray him.

I can't turn my back on her.

Bragg presses a button on his WristTop.

The Mark IX roars to life, shaking the surrounding ravine. Running lights across the outside of the fighter illuminate the immediate area. Its belly thrusters levitate it from the ground.

Bragg slides down the wall of the ravine and stands below the fighter. Showered in white light, his body is pulled upward into the Mark IX. The lower hatch slides open and suddenly Bragg is sitting in the cockpit's bucket seat.

The clear canopy provides a 360-degree view of the area. His feet rest on stiff pedals. Two parallel screens sit in front of the bulky control stick. The screens flicker on, along with the rest of the dim cockpit lighting.

MINERVA greets Bragg with a motherly, feminine voice. *"WELCOME BACK, COMMANDER."*

"I'm not a Commander anymore."

"AH, SO YOU'VE SAID. WHAT BRINGS YOU BACK?"

"I need some information. What happens to a person after they are arrested in Meridian?"

"NEW INMATES ARE TAKEN TO CENTRAL LOCKUP, TO AWAIT TRANSPORT TO THE LUNAR PENAL COLONY."

The sheer number of Enforcers would make it impossible for Bragg to rescue Dawn from the moon. "Show me the schedule to transport an inmate named Dawn Kheela."

"MAKING FRIENDS, I SEE. NOT THE GOOD KIND, IF SHE IS ON HER WAY TO THE LUNAR PENAL COLONY ..."

"I'm wanted across the galaxy. Can't be too judgy these days."

MINERVA does as instructed, speaking with what seems to be a jealous tone. *"A FAIR POINT, COMMANDER. THE ROCKET SET TO CARRY YOUR FELONIOUS FRIEND LEAVES IN THE MORNING. FEBRUARY 10, 2122 AT 0800."*

There is no time to waste.

Bragg removes his spare laser pistol from beneath his seat and pulls the padded leather harness over his shoulders. He begins to check the instruments and gauges surrounding him, in routine fashion.

Landing gear. Charge gauge. Flight controls. Engine idle. And weapons.

"IF YOU ARE THINKING WHAT I BELIEVE YOU ARE THINKING, MAY I SUGGEST TRANSFERRING ME TO YOUR WRISTTOP?"

Bragg taps his WristTop against the right screen, transferring the artificial intelligence as suggested. After finishing his pre-launch check, he reaches over to the left of the cockpit and grabs a stubby lever. He moves it upward. His seat starts to shake so forcefully it rattles his body.

The fighter rises from its hiding place until it hovers above the desolate surface, alone in the middle of nothing. The full moon takes up a lot of the night sky. Meridian's lights glow against the dark backdrop.

Bragg changes the right display screen with a swipe of his index finger, finally stopping at the navigation chart. MINERVA inputs the coordinates for central lockup.

Bragg takes the control stick into his hands and feels the familiar, gentle vibration. He presses down on the pedals beneath his feet. The thrusters ignite and send the fighter barreling across the dusty plain.

-----

4. The Forces of the Universe
"Killing isn't something you want on your conscience."

The squad car shudders as it makes its way through traffic. Dawn sits in the backseat behind two broad shouldered Enforcers. Her hands are lying in her lap, cuffed so tightly it hurts her wrists. She is only wearing her baggy black t-shirt.

Although she has encountered Enforcers before, this is her first time being arrested. The impending doom crushes her.

No one even knows where I am.

There is a clear screen divider between Dawn and the Enforcer's front seats. The Enforcers carry on a casual conversation, ignoring Dawn. Both are wearing traditional black uniforms with gold epaulettes. One drives as the other scrolls through a pornographic website on his WristTop.

Typical.

Dawn had never been able to overcome her frustration with life. Anytime she finally worked up the courage, and the means, to escape her situation, the forces of the universe always dragged her back.

Maybe I'm not allowed to want better.

Dawn knocks her head against the screen divider, producing a faint, repeating thud.

"Hey, back there! Cut that shit out!" the driver demands.

"Where are you takin' me?" Dawn asks.

She receives no answer. The passenger-side Enforcer has a perverted grin that raises his freckled cheeks. His hair is red, with a square cut. His eyes are dark black. He grabs the crotch of his uniform pants as he looks Dawn up and down.

Her body is riddled with chills from his piercing stare.

"My name is Omar. I think you would like me if you got to know me," he says, smiling.

"I doubt it," she replies.

Dawn can feel the hover car begin to slow down. They are exiting Meridian city limits. The highway narrows into a two-lane road and the metropolis is replaced with dusty plains.

"We will ask you again: Where is Samuel Bragg?" the driver demands.

"You know he is wanted, right? A half million credits to whoever knows his location." Omar flips his WristTop screen from lusty images to a wanted poster and shows it to Dawn. It has Bragg's face with "500,000" printed below.

The figure appears boldly to Dawn, to the point that it is all she can see.

That's five times more than I had stashed in the coffee can.

In an instant, her gripe with the universe vanishes. Dawn suddenly has the opportunity to turn the worst night of her life into the best day.

Dawn writhes in her seat. She has been called a lot of things, but a snitch is not one of them.

The hardest code to break is the one we hold ourselves to.

That is what Franklin taught her. Rule #1 of the Art of Villainy is "no snitching."

Now there is Bragg. The renegade pilot that chose to help her. There is something about Bragg that makes double crossing him difficult.

"I don't know who the fuck that is!" Dawn shouts.

"You don't want to tell us where the pilot is? Fine. To Central Lockup it is," the driver states.

Thirty or so minutes pass before the road dead ends into a solid metal gate. A monstrous building towers before them. It is built of cement and has two-foot-wide windows on each floor with bars over them.

The gate opens and allows the squad car to enter. The Enforcers exit and fling open the back door. Dawn steps out, her bare feet are numb from being cramped in the backseat. She is marched through the building's entrance, shoved through winding hallways, and taken to a booking area. There are rows of desks with wooden chairs next to them. Dawn is forced to sit in one.

After Dawn answers questions regarding her vitals, Enforcers take her photo and collect her fingerprints. When the cuffs are finally removed, blood rushes back into her hands and causes them to ache.

Dawn is then taken to a dark, dungeon-like basement. Two petite female guards, with black uniforms and matching hair buns, stand waiting for her.

"Step forward," orders one of the guards.

"Take off that t-shirt," says the other.

She does not move, as if remaining still will make the guards go away.

"Step forward!" the first one shouts. "And take off the t-shirt!"

Dawn begins trembling. She finally pulls the shirt over her head and tosses it at them.

She feels exposed. It's not the same as when she is dancing. At The Office, Dawn is unstoppable. Now, with nothing to shield her from the unwanted inspection, Dawn's vulnerability seeps from her pores.

One of the petite guards stamps the back of Dawn's hand with a number: *799261*. A short-sleeved jumpsuit is shoved into her arms. It's baggy and olive green, reeking of old sweat. The material is stale and rough on her skin.

Dawn is taken up a steep stairwell for what seems like one hundred floors. She hangs on to the wobbly side rail, pulling herself up at each step. The walls are beige and moldy.

Eventually they exit the stairwell and come out to a floor where holding cells line both sides of the hallway. Each cell has a transparent force field door with red tint. The ceiling is low. The air is stagnant.

Sweat soaks through the armpits of Dawn's green jumpsuit. As she is escorted, Dawn notices the person in each cell: men and women, drained of hope.

A guard pushes Dawn into a cell and then activates the force field behind her. The floor greets Dawn with a cold kiss. The cell is so tiny it suffocates her. It has a flickering, padded light on the ceiling. A single person bed is against the wall. A combination sink/toilet is in the corner.

Dawn lies down on the bed and stares up at the ceiling. Springs from the hard mattress poke at her back.

A night dancing at The Office doesn't sound so bad anymore.

Dawn thinks of Bragg. She thinks of Europa and its endless possibilities, impossible to reach now.

Despite the uncomfortable bed, exhaustion eventually wins out. Dawn falls asleep.

She dreams of her grandmother's house, specifically her old room. The creaky fan is rotating above as Dawn lies on her bed staring at it. Psych – Rock is blaring from speakers sitting on her nightstand. She bounces her foot to the rhythm of the music and smiles, taking it in. Shades on the room's window are open, letting in the pleasant day.

It is my favorite kind of afternoon.

Dawn is jarred back into reality. The ceiling fan is replaced with a dormant padded light. She is showered in sweat.

Two prisoners appear above her. One has long, unkempt hair. The other is bald with demon-like eyes. Both are burly with the sleeves torn off their jumpsuits. They crowd every inch of the space around Dawn's bed.

Dawn freezes, hoping this is just another dream. Or nightmare.

The moment she moves, the men grab her by the arms and legs. Dawn scratches and claws, but she can't stop them from dragging her from the bed. She yells and screams but the guards outside the cell do nothing but watch.

Dawn bites the hand of the bald captor. He lets out a flurry of profanities and responds with a violent smack to her face. The blow disorients her. The entire right side of her face stings as the outside world fades to black.

Once she regains consciousness, Dawn finds herself sitting in the corner of the cell next to the sink/toilet. The taste of blood stains her tongue. Her arms are purple from bruises.

The two prisoners from before are standing over her. Dawn attempts to get up but the long-haired prisoner pushes her down, slamming her into the wall. Her body throbs with soreness, like it has been dragged behind a hover truck.

A familiar laugh comes from behind the prisoners. They move aside and Omar, the Enforcer, steps into the cell with a shit eating grin.

"Today is our lucky day. Thanks boys," Omar says to the prisoners.

The prisoners smile at each other, and then proceed to tear Dawn's jumpsuit off. Their hands forcefully grasp her body. She tries to push the men off but every attempt is met with a punch to the face.

Her cheeks pulsate as they swell.

There is no way out.

Once the top of her jumpsuit is torn off, cold air meets Dawn's bare breasts. The prisoners hold her legs open as Omar walks towards them, unbuckling his belt.

The closer Omar gets, the more it feels like this is happening to someone else. Dawn places herself on the opposite side of the cell, as another person, watching the horror about to unfold.

Suddenly everything is plunged into total darkness. The force field door malfunctions and Dawn realizes that the electricity has failed.

She tries to push herself up but is still pinned by the prisoners. Yells echo through the hall.

"What do we do?" one of the prisoners asks.

"Keep holding her down. I'm not waiting any longer. I don't care what's going on," Omar says.

Dawn can't make anything out in the dark. Her thighs are held open firmly. She quivers, anticipating the unwanted penetration that could come at any second.

This can't be happening.

A flurry of blue laser bolts interrupts the darkness. The prisoners fall and are slumped over Dawn. A few moments pass. Then someone pulls the prisoners off and helps Dawn to her feet. What remains of her jumpsuit falls to the floor around her ankles.

The emergency power kicks on, providing dim red lighting that flashes on and off. Naked, Dawn struggles to hide her body with her arms. She fears this person wants what Omar wanted.

The man steps forward as the light flashes, revealing his identity.

Bragg.

Dawn forms her mouth to say something, but is so flustered nothing comes out. She falls toward Bragg, wrapping him in a hug. He is real.

But this must be a dream.

Before she can speak, Dawn spots Omar scurrying from the cell. He is whimpering with his pants around his ankles.

Mr. Rapist ain't so tough without his posse.

"You son of a bitch!" Dawn screams, at the top of her lungs. She grabs Omar by the leg before he can escape and pulls him back into the cell.

Bragg comes up beside her and points a laser pistol at the Enforcer.

"Let me do it," Dawn says.

There is a long pause. Bragg hesitates. "Killing isn't something you want on your conscience."

"I've seen plenty of death!" Dawn protests.

"Seeing it is one horrible thing. Doing it yourself is another."

Rage oozes through Dawn, finding no climax when Bragg squeezes the trigger. Her eyes stay fixated on Omar. Each kick of the pistol startles her, but does not deter her from watching. The rounds burn half of Omar's face into char.

Bragg then turns to Dawn. His gaze is sharp. Grey eyes pierce into her soul. She takes a few steps backward, instinctively putting distance between them.

"What . . . What's wrong?" Dawn asks.

"Do you want to live?" Bragg replies. His voice is monotone and direct, and much more dominant than before.

"What do you mean?" Dawn says.

Bragg steps toward her, cupping her cheeks in the palms of his hands. They are coarse on her skin. His voice echoes in her ears as he says, "Don't look at what is going on around us. It's best you don't see."

"TIME TO GET A MOVE ON, COMMANDER. ENFORCERS HAVE DISPATCHED REINFORCEMENTS."

The female voice came from Bragg's WristTop. "Who is that?" Dawn asks.

"Let's go. Keep up," Bragg orders, taking her by the hand.

Dawn follows Bragg from the cell without resistance, being led like a child. He holds her hand with a firm grip, pulling her along.

Everything in the crowded hallway is moving in slow motion. Dawn is in a trance.

Snap out of it, D! This is really happening.

Red emergency lights flash on and off overhead. The intermittent tint reveals brief glimpses of carnage, alternating the grim scene on and off. Barbaric yells bring Dawn back to reality. She is nude and unsafe. Guards brawl with the prisoners all around her.

Red flash. Dawn can see a splatter of blood on the floor.

Darkness.

Red flash. A face appears to her left, wide mouthed, screaming.

Darkness.

Red flash. Large hands emerge and grasp at Dawn.

Darkness.

Red Flash. Dawn becomes smothered in a sea of tussling bodies. Her hand is ripped away from Bragg's. She can see less and less of him as he disappears into the crowd.

Darkness.

Red flash. Dawn can see Bragg further ahead now, in a grapple with a guard.

Darkness.

A loud explosion shakes the building. Laser rounds flare through the air, sending both prisoners and guards fleeing for their lives.

Darkness.

Red flash. Bragg returns for Dawn. Behind him, Dawn can see Villains, clad in their signature royal blue and black. They fight with the prisoners and the guards, adding to the bedlam.

Darkness.

Red flash. Bragg grasps Dawn, leading her through the chaos. He cups her head with his large palm, holding it down as they are jostled around by the surrounding uproar.

Darkness.

Red flash. They burst through a doorway, arriving in the moldy stairwell. Dawn and Bragg turn and find themselves on the bad end of three laser pistols.

Darkness.

Suddenly, the electricity is restored. The lighting returns to normal. Dawn and Bragg are on a landing in the stairwell. Zin Alpha, or *"The Doctor,"* is standing in front of them. He has buzzed blond hair. His blue eyes peek over boxy shades. A royal blue vest fits snug across his chest. Three gold chains drape his neck.

Behind him are three Villain henchmen wearing royal blue hoodies. Each of the henchmen is pointing a firearm.

"Whoa! Where are you off to?" Zin asks. He looks more closely at Dawn. "Wait, isn't this one of ours? Why are you naked? Are you even working the prisoners?"

The three Villain henchmen laugh.

Dawn has never liked the Doctor. "I thought you came with Bragg," she says.

"We were hired to kill a snitch," says Zin. "The newswire said Central Lockup's power is malfunctioning, so we piled into a carrier and hurried over."

"I'm the reason the power went out. I came to get you alone," Bragg says to Dawn.

Alone?

Dawn stares at the pilot. He is firm in his conviction.

"Is that your Space Force fighter buzzing around the sky outside?" Zin asks, finally signaling for the Villains to lower their pistols. "I didn't know civilians owned fighters. Or that fighters could fly themselves."

"They don't. And most can't," Bragg replies coldly.

"I see," says Zin. "You better come with us, space boy. Franklin will want to talk."

"I'd rather not."

Zin glances back at the three Villains. "Take him."

They move to grab hold of Bragg, but before they can get their hands on him Dawn throws herself between them and Bragg. "Back off!" she cries.

The henchmen shove Dawn aside. She watches as Bragg takes one step toward the first attacker and strikes him in the nose with a jab. A *crack* reverberates up the stairwell before the Villain cries out and falls to his knees. Blood spills from his nostrils and down onto his hoodie. The other two henchmen are hesitant to come to his aid.

Several other Villains enter the stairwell from the chaos-filled hallway. It takes seven of them to wrestle Bragg down.

Dawn jumps in, planting her feet and using all the strength she has to pull the henchmen off the pilot. She resorts to scratching and biting them before Zin grabs her.

Dawn and Bragg have their wrists bound. The Villains escort them to Central Lockup's rooftop, where an egg-shaped hover carrier is waiting idly.

As they are seated aboard, Dawn is grateful to at least be headed home.

-----

5. The Art of Villainy
"The real question is, who are the heroes?"

Bragg stands in a cul-de-sac, looking upon a dilapidated mansion. The structure sits up on a hill, behind a rusted iron fence. Its grey brick is worn. The place looks abandoned, along with the other estates in the neighborhood.

A group wearing royal blue and black clothing surrounds Bragg. His hands are bound in front of him.

There is no way to escape.

Dawn stands close to him. She is barefoot, draped in a borrowed blue sweater and sweat pants. Her face is battered but she is seemingly unbothered by their situation.

"I think they've made a mistake," Bragg whispers to Dawn.

"Nope. This is the place," she tells him.

The group starts up the cracked driveway that winds along the left side of the hill. Bragg is urged along by those behind him. He reasons if these people wanted to kill him, they would have done so already.

The entrance to the mansion has a lofty ebony door with a stone gargoyle on each side.

The monstrous sculptures have bat-like wings and bare fangs from snarling mouths. They shadow the dooryard, shimmering under the sunlight with a subtle, eerie aura of life.

Waist-high hedges line a path from the driveway to the door. Two men guard the entrance, both wearing royal blue jumpsuits that taper at the waist. As the group approaches, the pair flash a hand sign by extending their ring and middle finger to form a "V." They then step aside and grant entry.

Past the doorway lies a stark contrast to the mansion's exterior. Everything is renovated and exquisitely decorated. Bragg and Dawn are marched down a golden arched hallway with tan tile floors. Hanging on the walls are expensive paintings in the Renaissance style, all displayed in hand-crafted frames.

The hallway opens to a brilliant foyer. The domed ceiling is painted with a mural of individuals dressed in royal blue and black formal wear, sprawled out in artistic poses. Bragg almost falls backward admiring it. The detail is surreal with vibrant hues and seamless brushstrokes.

U-shaped stairs curve up the walls of the foyer to a second story. The group leads Bragg and Dawn straight, taking them through a corridor beneath the stairs. It opens to a sizable, crowded kitchen. Everyone is dressed in suits and pencil skirts, all with royal blue and black color patterns. Bragg's dingy white undershirt stands out.

The kitchen is fit for a Martian movie star. A checkered backsplash surrounds the space. A massive marble island lies in the middle with a full assortment of polished, stainless-steel cookware hanging above.

Eyes turn to Bragg as he is escorted through the crowd. The glares are aggressive. He is outnumbered thirty to one, at best. Bragg's stroll becomes less confident. Dawn moves closer to him, enough to gently brush his hand. This comforts him.

The kitchen is open to a den where people sit around makeshift card tables. Plush couches lie in front of two mounted screens, each split into various sporting events. The card games are rowdy, with the players consuming synthetic alcohol and heckling each other.

Bragg and Dawn are marched right through the people sitting and enjoying themselves. The head captor leans over toward Bragg. "I don't think I told you before, my name is Doctor Zin Alpha."

A doctor? In a space gang?

Zin pushes his shades up onto his nose, looking Dawn up and down. "Is Dawn your girlfriend, pilot?" he asks, announcing his question so the entire room hears it. "You're dating a legend. I mean, she's 'dated' everyone at this point!"

Others around them laugh, adding jeers and rude comments. Bragg looks over at Dawn. Her contused cheeks are bright red. Her mean stare unsuccessfully hides the discomfort caused by the comment.

"Suppose she dumped you for being an asshole," Bragg retorts, louder than he anticipated.

The rowdy room quells. The sly comment has soured the mood. Bragg can feel his temper slipping, but focuses on maintaining a calm exterior.

Zin's face tightens. "Watch yourself. Hate for us to get off on the wrong foot."

"I was thinking the same thing," Bragg says.

The twelve or so goons stand down from their games, gradually approaching Bragg. The others from the kitchen begin to surround them as well.

Dawn steps in front of Bragg. "You're going to fight him with his hands zip tied?" she shouts, glaring at Zin.

The goons have mischievous grins as they crack their knuckles. Attention from the entire room squeezes Bragg. His eyes dart around the room, planning to make an example out of the first attacker.

"Didn't you say Franklin is waiting?" Dawn says to Zin. "We can't put off the boss."

Grudgingly, Zin raises his hand. The goons back away. Zin leads Bragg and Dawn through the corridor and back out to the domed foyer. The three of them ascend the stairs to the second story, where Zin opens a door on the right and then motions for Bragg to enter.

Bragg stops in front of the door, certain now that the Villains plan to collect the Union's reward. He turns and studies the doctor.

But Zin offers no clue as to what lies inside. He just glares at Bragg with displeasure. "Come on. I don't have all day!"

Bragg steps through the doorway. Dawn follows him. The doctor tries to stop her, but she shoves him away hard and goes inside.

Bragg and Dawn stand side by side and look around. The room is an odd, darkened study. Bookshelves full of ancient hardback books line the walls. There is no other furniture.

A man sits atop a silk blue pillow on the floor, with his legs crossed. He has dreadlocked hair that is starting to grey. His beard is neatly trimmed. A fire crackles in the giant fireplace behind him, providing warmth and the only source of light.

The man is dressed like a politician, wearing a white dress shirt and blue necktie.

Suspenders hold up his pants and round shades hide his eyes. A scar runs across his left brow.

An alien female stands next to the dreadlocked man. She is muscular with ghost white skin. Short teal hair is slicked back over her head. Her teal eyes are fixed on Bragg. She wears a black corset covered by a slim-fitting black jacket. Fangs barely show through her full lips.

"Please come in," the dreadlocked man says. He has a deep voice. "My name is Franklin. Franklin Hendrix."

A sly grin curls Franklin's mouth as he motions up to the alien. "This rare gem is from the Alpha Centauri system. Her name is Shea Shibaz. But you must call her The Queen."

Franklin stands up from the pillow. He looks toward the fire, then back at Bragg. He rubs his hands together as if trying to warm them. The flames reflect off his shades, giving them a sharp glare. "So, my guess is you're an Earthling. You lied about being age eighteen and ran off to join the Space Force. How did you end up trying to save our working girl from the Enforcers?"

Franklin knows more than he is letting on. No sense dancing around it. "Got out of the Space Force early. Difference of opinions," Bragg responds.

Franklin's face gradually morphs into a smile. Then he laughs so heartily it seems to shake the room. He slaps his hand on his thigh.

Bragg maintains his neutral expression.

"Everyone should have an opinion different from the Union!" Franklin says, as his laughter finally dies down.

Bragg continues. "I visited The Office. A group crashed in and shot the place up. Dawn helped me escape, but got arrested later."

"Must have been some dance," Franklin chuckles, glaring at Dawn. "Why not just leave her and go on about your life?"

"It didn't seem right to abandon her."

"Well, that's noble. But chivalry gets you killed in this game, youngster. I'm glad we were able to assist you this time, but I wouldn't make that a habit."

Franklin's demeanor is calming. Some of his words are grandiose.

"I'm not in 'this game'," Bragg replies.

"Your loyalty to Dawn is impressive," says Franklin. "I fear few in our gang would display such devotion as you have for her. However, it is a lot of effort for a working girl. How much do you really know about her?"

Bragg finds the question odd. He doesn't ask Franklin to elaborate, but it follows anyway.

"Dawn is beautiful. But . . . she is a working girl. They can be manipulative. She does not have the best reputation for honesty."

"Fuck you," Dawn mumbles from beside Bragg.

"Why did you capture me?" Bragg interrupts.

"Straight to the point. Because I'd like you to join the Villains."

"Who are the Villains?"

"The real question is, who are the heroes? Gangs everywhere are trying to take over. The Villains aren't much, yet, but we are family. We own The Office," Franklin says, a sense of pride in his voice. "And The Office was undermanned last night because a bunch of Villains have been killed by the Asteroids, a rival gang from Comet City. They're new blood trying to push us out."

"Why do you want me to join your gang? And do I really have a choice?" Bragg asks, holding up his bound hands.

Franklin motions to The Queen, who walks over to Bragg. The Queen is beautiful but terrifying up close. She towers over him. Her skin is smooth and unblemished like porcelain. Her ears are slightly pointed at the ends. Her teal eyes are brimming with madness.

She cuts the binds from his hands with a lighting-fast swipe of her claw-like nails. She scowls at Dawn, slices her binds with the same motion, and then returns to stand beside Franklin.

"I can tell you live for a good fight," Franklin continues. "We could help each other. The Villains will ensure the Union never gets to you. Or you can leave and take your chances alone."

Bragg fears Franklin is right. He misses the fight. That is the tricky thing about war; while fighting, the biggest enemy is fatigue. A pilot's stomach weakens as the death toll rises. However, when the war is over, and the killing is done, it's all a pilot longs for. "What do the Villains do, exactly?" he asks.

"We participate in minuscule vices. We dabble in gambling, exotic clubs, and pandering."

"You follow no rules?"

"The Art of Villainy. Our own set of rules."

Sweat forms above Bragg's brow. Even considering joining a gang seems farfetched. But there is something about Franklin that Bragg admires. The proposal hangs in the air for an eternity.

"I don't plan to stay on Earth long. I promised Dawn I'd take her to Europa."

Dawn snaps her head around toward Bragg. Her eyes are wide and the color drains from her swollen face. She tries to surreptitiously shake her head, but their captors notice.

The Queen frowns, becoming visibly angry.

"Remain calm, beautiful Queen," says Franklin. "This will be dealt with."

She ignores Franklin, as if he said nothing at all, continuing to stare a hole through Bragg's forehead. Her stance is tense, as if she will lunge forward at any moment.

"Composure, Shea," Franklin says. "Composure."

Bragg grows concerned about her apparent aggression when, this time, the Queen flashes her fangs.

What is her deal?

Franklin turns to Bragg. "Europa?"

"Yes," he replies, keeping his eyes on the alien.

"Interesting," Franklin continues. "Science says it's inhabitable. However, I've heard there is an alien race living there. Supposedly they have a lake that the natives use to stay young forever."

"I suppose it's possible."

"Well, you are free to go whenever you like. However, why don't you help with the Asteroids until you leave? In exchange for the protection we offer?"

Being freed in exchange for service does not seem much like freedom. However, given the circumstances, Bragg finds the proposal agreeable. Not having to worry about the Union would give him more energy to find a way to Europa.

"There is one more thing," Franklin says, after a moment. "Taking Dawn to Europa might be an issue. She is The Queen's girl."

"Wait… Dawn and Shea are dating?" Bragg's unrealized hopes are suddenly dashed.

The Queen scoffs. "It's 'The Queen!' she replies. "And the working girl belongs to me."

The Queen has a distinct high-pitched voice, accented by clicking and hissing. It unsettles Bragg. He has never encountered her race of aliens before.

"So . . . she is a slave?" Bragg asks.

"It's more employee – employer," Franklin says.

Dawn lets out a vexatious chuckle. She fidgets and shakes her head at Bragg, who studies her.

She is afraid.

"Then Dawn should quit," Bragg adds.

"That's not how we work, Uni," Franklin replies.

"People should be free to do as they please," Bragg says boldly. "Otherwise, you might as well be the Union."

Dawn moves closer to Bragg. Her face is now full of determination and her fists are balled up. "I agree."

"Don't let tis Uni fuck up yer head, bitch," The Queen snarls.

Franklin laughs nervously, placing his hand on the alien's broad shoulder. The Queen is sneering. "She just means why not continue to dance? With your beauty and skill, I'm sure it will continue to be lucrative."

"No. I said what I meant," The Queen injects.

"I want more out of life," Dawn replies.

There is a brief pause in the conversation. Bragg locks eyes with Dawn, and nods. "Is Dawn not free to leave?" he presses.

"No, she ain't," The Queen says. "Find someone else to take to yer fantasy world!"

"If it wasn't for him, I'd be on the way to the fucking moon!" Dawn yells.

"Everyone. Calm yourselves," Franklin says.

"I will help with your Asteroid problem until I find a way to Europa. As long as you let Dawn come with me when I leave," Bragg blurts.

"No!" The Queen shouts.

Franklin turns and stares into the crackling fire. He looks back at The Queen, and then at Dawn. "You have a deal, Uni. But she has to continue to work at The Office in the meantime."

"What the fuck do yer mean?" The Queen exclaims.

"We will talk later, Shea," Franklin says to the upset alien.

"Deal," Dawn adds, motioning towards Bragg to agree.

"Fine," Bragg echoes.

"Dawn, darling. Go with the Doctor. I want you to help the others with cleaning up The Office," Franklin says. "As for you, Uni, you can stay here for tonight – but no longer. Not until you've earned some stripes."

"I understand," Bragg replies. He and Dawn turn and leave the study.

In a moment they are standing alone just outside the door to Franklin's study. "That was intense!" Dawn says.

"Why?" Bragg asks.

"Because they are dangerous, especially The Queen. You have no idea."

"Is that why you are trying to flee this employer-employee relationship?" Bragg asks.

Dawn steps back from Bragg. She averts her eyes from his, looking down and to the side. Her voice softens. "That stuff Franklin said . . ."

The Doctor approaches, coming up the stairs beside them, disturbing the conversation.

"Franklin said you need a ride to The Office," Zin says, looking at Dawn.

"In a second. I'm talking," Dawn replies, glaring at him.

"Finish your discussion later. The pilot has something waiting for him downstairs," Zin says.

Bragg peers over the second story railing. In the foyer below are ten of the goons from before. They all have the sleeves of their dress shirts rolled up and they all look up at him with a menacing glare.

"Would you just drop it?" Dawn asks. "Are you really still on about that?"

"No one cares about that shit from earlier," Zin says. "I already know what Franklin wants with him. This is initiation."

"But there are . . ."

Bragg stops Dawn. "It's fine."

I live for a good fight.

Bragg underwent a similar ceremony as a cadet in the Space Force. It was a tradition ignored by command and a ritual held secret among the noncommissioned.

To be accepted, you must prove your toughness.

Bragg starts down the stairs to the foyer. A sweeping leg kick takes the first attacker off his feet. Bragg manages to incapacitate six or so of the men before he is finally overwhelmed.

The remaining gang holds Bragg down. Endless feet pound him as they stomp.

I've had worse.

-----

6. The Queen
"Watch yer tone."

All Dawn can think about is Bragg. She wants to explore her developing connection with the pilot. However, the longer she imagines possibilities, the more she convinces herself it won't work. Bragg emits a gallantry Dawn fears she'll taint.

Stick to the plan and use him to escape Earth.

Zin takes Dawn to The Office and drops her off. Upon arrival, she is tasked with helping the Villains clean up the club for reopening. Dawn grabs a broom and begins to sweep the floor behind the bar. She finds a full flask of Martian vodka and decides to keep it for herself.

Dawn thinks of Europa and what it must be like.

Gold paved streets? Beautiful weather?

She returns her focus to sweeping the broken glass. Dawn rewards her efforts at forming each pile with a swig from the flask.

The Queen enters through the opaque door. A black corset and latex pants hug her frame. Her long legs give her a powerful stride. Her pale face has light makeup.

Dawn tenses up.

The Queen frowns at the sight of her, as if suddenly disgusted.

Dawn prepares to be scolded, beaten, or worse.

However, The Queen does not approach her. She takes a seat at the only remaining table and ignores everyone.

After a day of clean-up work, The Office begins to resemble its former self. The sun sets, handing the sky over to the moon.

The Queen has remained in her seat the entire day.

Dawn can tell her mood is sour, as it often is. Already inebriated with vodka, Dawn takes a couple of Martian ales from behind the bar. She sits down next to The Queen, opens one of the ales, and slides it across the table to her.

"Who told yer to leave with some Uni pilot?" The Queen says.

"I'm sorry . . . I was going to tell you . . ." Dawn stammers.

"Tell? Yer don't tell me shite, bitch. Yer ask." The Queen says.

"Please . . ." Dawn says. "I have been loyal to you for years. But I'm tired and I want something more than this life."

"What are yer hoping to find on Europa?"

"Something better."

"I'm sad to hear that. That what I provide is not enough."

"No . . . you know I don't mean it that way . . ."

"I mean, who could blame yer! Look at tis menial bullshit Franklin has me doing. Tis beneath me!" The Queen laments.

Fortunately, Dawn views rebuilding The Office as a chance to prove herself to the gang. She sips some of the ale and explains her perspective to The Queen. "I know I can help get this place going again," Dawn says.

"Good luck. The dancers were captured by Asteroids during the last shootin'. Last I heard they are either pimping 'em out or forcing 'em to dance in their 'go-go' club," The Queen replies.

Forced? I know them. We are colleagues. Destiny. Crystal. Even Imani. I don't like her because she stole from me once, but still… I can only imagine what it must be like for them. Forced to do things, unimaginable things, against their will.

Dawn shivers, feeling the ghost of Omar's breath on the nape of her neck. "Why didn't you say this before?" she cries, jumping up from the seat and raising her voice with liquid courage. "We have to help them!"

The Queen seems unbothered, taking a swig of her ale. "Would be less hassle to just get new dancers. The Asteroids would never part with the girls without a fight."

Awful. She'll never feel the way I do about this. But I also know what motivates her.

"Since when are you worried about a fight against such 'weaklings'?" Dawn says, mocking The Queen's accent.

"Watch yer tone," The Queen warns sternly.

"Just saying. It would be a lot more interesting than clean up duty." Dawn reaches across the table and lightly brushes The Queen's arm.

The Queen's mouth curves into a grin.

Dawn is not so sure it doesn't look sinister.

"Fine. We'll go help yer colleagues. First, help me with something out back."

Dawn's stomach sinks. Here comes *the catch*. She follows The Queen through the dressing room and out to the alley behind the club.

A luxury hover car sits idle, floating alone in the alley. The Queen walks to the front and opens the trunk. Inside is a man, gagged and hogtied. His orange hoodie is drenched in blood. He screams, muffled, at the sight of The Queen.

"Tis is the Asteroid that told me about the dancers," The Queen says.

"If he told you, why do you still have him tied up?" Dawn asks.

"Yer right . . ."

The Queen laughs uncontrollably. She pushes Dawn aside and uses her razor-sharp fingernails to claw flesh off the man's body in chunks. He wails in pain, stifled by the gag. Blood is everywhere, sprayed across The Queen's face and chest.

"No! NO! I meant, let him go!" Dawn shouts.

The Queen does not reply. She steps back, continuing to stare down at the squirming man. "Yer a disloyal bitch. I found the stash of credits hidden in yer apartment. Tis plan to leave started before yer met space boy."

Dawn stumbles backwards. There is nothing she can say to defend herself. The Queen continues speaking without looking up.

"Kill tis Rock and prove yer are still loyal to me." The Queen removes a knife from her jacket and hands it to Dawn.

"Please. No, I will stay here and I will pay you back whatever . . ."

"Shut up! Tis is what I want. Kill 'im. Or I'll kill yer pilot boyfriend."

Dawn's gut is on fire. Her legs are shaky. The thought of taking a life sends a tremble through her body.

Bragg was right. It is different.

Hesitant, Dawn weighs each heavy step toward the open trunk. The closer she gets, the more she hears the Asteroid's muffled screams. She takes the sharpened knife from The Queen and stares at the blade.

I can't let her kill Bragg. He would do this for me.

"Finish him," The Queen demands. She steps away from the trunk, covered from forehead to knees in blood.

He is suffering at this point. It's just putting him out of his misery.

Dawn turns the knife blade side down and jabs it into the man. It enters beneath his ribcage. He screams in pain, squirming in the trunk violently, shaking the hover car. Dawn plunges the knife into the man one last time, this time aimed at his heart.

The screaming finally stops.

The Queen turns to Dawn. "Yer aren't going anywhere. The pilot, nor anyone else, can care fer yer like I do."

"And how do you care for me?" Dawn asks, still in a state of shock.

"Yer are dressed in the highest fashion and dined on the finest foods, yer ungrateful bitch!" The Queen snarls. "The pilot has nothing to offer yer!"

It becomes apparent that The Queen's anger towards Bragg stems from jealousy.

"You don't care for me. What he has to offer is genuine. Maybe I don't deserve that."

"Yer don't. Stay away from the pilot. If yer don't come to yer senses, I'll remove him from the equation."

The Queen's face is emotionless, looking almost inanimate. Dawn has witnessed The Queen kill, bare handed. Her temper is as hot as her appearance. Her viciousness knows no bounds. The Queen's resentment of Bragg could put him in danger if not quelled.

Dawn speaks nervously. "Please don't. I understand. I was just using the pilot to get off the planet. I don't care for him . . . not like I care for you."

7. Franklin
"You need clothes. You are a Villain now."

Venturing from the Villains' mansion the following day, Bragg walks with Franklin at a leisurely pace. The sun is pleasant, warming everything it touches. Bragg takes in each abandoned estate along the route. Each one is an ancient monument to wealth with boards covering the windows. Graffiti is splattered across the sides. Brilliant fountains and sculptures displayed in the front yards are now decayed.

Parting with the silence that has carried them, Franklin looks to Bragg and motions to the structures around them. "The depression in 2082 hit this area hard. People lost their jobs, then their homes. Many took their own lives. Materialism can be a person's demise."

Bragg takes Franklin as an intellectual, but not someone studied in books or schools. Franklin is someone wise from experience. The scar across his left brow hints at his hardened past. At least a decade older than Bragg, Franklin uses brilliant language and relatable metaphors.

"I grew up on Earth during the First Interplanetary War, in the days before the Union." Franklin explains somberly. "It was a time when Earth fought to remain free of Mars. After my older brother was drafted and killed in battle, I began to protest the vile war. When I turned age seventeen, I was sent to prison for refusing to enlist. Pa. Mother. Both killed while I was in prison. Casualties of war."

Bragg offers only short responses. Seeing the anguish in Franklin's face and hearing the sorrow in his tone disheartens Bragg. He knows deep down that he has caused many to feel the way Franklin does.

How many brothers, fathers, and sisters have I taken away?

"When I was released from the Lunar Penal Colony, the war was over. The Union won," Franklin continues. "I came back to Earth and started the Villains with some guys I met inside."

"You know . . ." Bragg struggles, tormented by guilt into brutal honesty. "During the Second Interplanetary War, I . . ."

"Of course, I know what you've done," Franklin interrupts.

Bragg pauses his walk, astonished by the comment.

Franklin places his hand on Bragg's shoulder and smiles a warm, parental grin. "You were indoctrinated as soon as you began schooling. 'Join the Union. Do your part!' But you left. Most don't."

The man is hardly what you would expect from a notorious gangster. A spark of forgiveness washes over Bragg, as if a tiny portion of his insurmountable sin has been absolved. Bragg begins to revel in a concocted idea that Franklin's forgiveness can somehow be imparted to the families of his victims.

"You need clothes. You are a Villain now," Franklin says.

"There is no need. As I said, I'm only on the planet temporarily."

"I insist," Franklin replies, "I know a place a few blocks from here. It is such a pleasant day, let's just walk there."

He leads Bragg to a local tailor in a standalone building on the edge of the city. The door chimes as they enter the upscale boutique. Racks of dress clothes form a lengthy aisle to the back of the store, where a man sits behind a counter.

The man looks up as Bragg and Franklin approach. His face lights up at the sight of them. He is short and stocky. He wears a well-tailored black suit and expensive-looking glasses. His teeth are bright, adding to the room. His hair is in a neat pompadour.

"Franklin, curse the Universe! I figured someone would have killed you by now," the man says, walking out from behind the counter.

"A lot have tried, Howard. A lot have tried," Franklin says.

They meet before the counter, laughing and embracing each other. Howard steps back from Franklin and then looks Bragg up and down. His smile slowly shifts to a frown and his laugh quells. "What's with the Uni?" Howard asks.

"How did you know?" Franklin asks, stunned.

"The way he stands. Tall, proper, military like," Howard replies.

"I see. Well . . . meet Samuel Bragg, deserter pilot," Franklin says. "He needs a suit."

"Deserter? Friend, that's suicide. Especially walking around with posture like that," Howard says to Bragg. "You are not very incognito."

Howard again looks Bragg over, then unenthusiastically thrusts out a hand.

Bragg shakes his cold but firm grip.

Howard motions for Bragg to follow him, leading them behind a curtain. Dress shirts are folded and placed on shelves along the walls. Tables line the room with A.I. operated sewing machines.

Howard takes a measuring tape and begins running it along Bragg's arms and torso. "How tall are you? Seventy-two inches? Seventy-three inches'?"

"Seventy-three," Bragg replies. "And a hundred and two kilograms."

A few minutes pass as Howard scurries around the room. He returns with a royal blue suit, precisely pressed. Bragg steps into the dressing room and removes his tattered clothing piece by piece.

Shrouding an old life, embracing a new one.

When Bragg comes out of the dressing room, he looks at himself in a nearby tri-fold mirror. The suit fits slim, like a glove to his frame. The jacket is lengthened to the middle of his abdomen. A skinny tie, matching the suit color, lay harmoniously down his black dress shirt. Bragg has never owned clothing made with such quality.

Howard continues to measure his pants, altering the bottom with laser trimmers. The trimmers cut the fabric ankle high to show most of his black boots.

"Something is missing," Franklin says. He takes a pair of dark sunglasses from a nearby table and places them on Bragg's face. "That's it."

"I think the Uni is set," Howard says.

"He also needs . . . other equipment," Franklin says to Howard.

"Ah. This way then," Howard says.

Howard pulls away a wool rug, revealing a hidden door in the floor. He opens the door, gaining access to a ladder. They all descend the ladder and arrive in a metallic bunker. Various handguns, rifles and other weapons hang on each wall. Metal chests litter the floor, making the area hard to maneuver in.

Bragg feels called to a pair of shiny silver ray guns, hanging parallel to each other. His reflection is pellucid on the sleek metal barrels. They are plain, with seamless muzzles, guards and hammers. The handles are grey.

Franklin walks up beside Bragg. "You like these?" Franklin asks.

"Of course he likes them," Howard laughs, peeking his head out from a chest and scurrying over. "The entire galaxy likes them! Those are twin Wolf Errickson ray guns. One of only twenty sets ever made."

When Howard takes one of the pistols from its place on the wall and aims it, the handle glows and produces a high-pitched whine.

"These kick like a cannon. Tough to wield for an amateur marksman," Howard presents, as if it's a challenge. "Even with the discount I'd give to Franklin . . . they are still five thousand credits."

Any and all fascination Bragg had with the rare guns diminishes with the announcement of the price tag. He looks at Franklin, who is smiling.

"I'll take them," Franklin says. "Bragg is going to take good care of them."

"No, thank you," Bragg says.

Gifts like that come with strings.

"No catch," Franklin states. "Besides, I'm only going to pay twenty-five hundred credits for them. Isn't that right, Howard?"

Franklin holds out his WristTop.

Howard hurries over with a tablet to scan away the credits. After the transaction is complete, Howard swiftly polishes the guns and hands them to Bragg.

Each gun is heavy to the touch. The three-inch barrels extend past his index finger. Bragg realizes he should give the ray guns back, but doesn't.

Materialism can be a person's demise.

"Hold it, kid," Howard says. "You are going to need somewhere to put those." He searches the chests scattered about the floor until he finds a black underarm harness with two holsters. "Genuine leather. Protects the barrels from wear."

"Do you have any hip holsters?" Bragg asks.

"Rule #4 of the Art of Villainy: Never advertise you're armed," Howard replies.

There is an eerie feeling in Bragg's gut. He is dressed head to toe in Villain colors as he and Franklin exit the tailor shop. The clothes make him feel taller. Beneath each armpit sits firearms worth two months of Space Force salary. Sooner or later, Bragg knows he will be ordered to use the ray guns.

To scare someone. To kill someone.

"Are you hungry? Let's grab some food," Franklin says.

As the duo make their way along the busy Meridian sidewalk, Bragg notices that every passing person looks him up and down. He no longer feels like trash.

Their trek brings them to a diner a few blocks west, just after dusk. The building resembles a shiny aluminum toaster. The specials are displayed in the windows, written with marker in big block letters.

A clarion chime sounds as Franklin pulls open the door. The establishment has booths with red seating along the window side. The flooring is white and black checkered tile. Countertop seating lies opposite the booths.

There is a commotion inside. Two males, both clad in ragged orange clothing, are intimidating the elderly couple behind the counter. One of the men is burly with olive-colored skin. His bald head drips sweat, glistening under the diner's sterile lighting. His mammoth hands pound the countertop.

The other skinnier man is wearing an orange coat that is too large for him. His hands are in the pockets. He shouts at the couple, "*Stop playing games! Pay up or else.*"

The elderly couple is holding each other. The old man is balding, with salt and pepper hair. He has a hunched back. The woman has a caramel complexion and short poofy hair. She is wearing wire frame glasses and reminds Bragg of his late mother.

Maybe it's the sunken, loving eyes.

Watching the terrorized couple brings Bragg's blood to a boil. He marches past Franklin. "Leave them alone," Bragg says sternly, once he is a few yards from the men.

The men pause, looking at each other, then at Bragg.

"Who the fuck is ye?" the burly guy asks.

"Why are you bullying these people?" Bragg replies, seething inside.

"We are the local security force. The Whitakers here are behind on payments." The skinny guy steps away from the counter and faces Bragg.

"The only protection they need is from you," Bragg says.

The skinny man removes his hands from his coat pockets and starts towards Bragg.

Once he is close enough to grab, Bragg delivers a quick kick to his gut.

The skinny man stumbles backward and rejoins his partner, coughing excessively. Both the men brandish laser knives: red beam energy blades with short handles.

Franklin lunges at the burly man, tackling him so hard he drops his blade.

The shop owners begin throwing things from behind the counter at the skinny man. He protects his head with his hands as the items bombard him, yelling at the couple to stop.

Bragg picks up the dropped laser knife while the skinny man is distracted and slices the man's shoulder.

He lets out a blood-curdling scream. Defeated, the two men scramble towards the exit and trip several times in their own haste.

Franklin starts after them. "Come on. Let's go!"

"They are gone. The matter is settled," Bragg replies. He can see the two men from the diner window, fleeing toward a black convertible hover car.

"Rule #2 of the Art of Villainy," Franklin says. "Never let a rival point a weapon at you twice."

"Take our hatchback," the older man says. He tosses a block shaped proximity key onto the countertop.

"The city is tired of these punks," the woman adds.

"Fine," Bragg agrees.

Bragg and Franklin find the hover hatchback behind the diner, parked under a single streetlight, showcasing the vehicle in the night. It is white with four doors. They climb inside. The engine revs and the hatchback hovers off the ground as Franklin zooms out of the parking lot.

Traffic is sparse, but Bragg begins to fear they've lost the Asteroids. He holds his WristTop to his mouth. "MINERVA. I need the location of a black hover car. Should be somewhere in front of me, likely driving erratically."

"Who are you talking to?" Franklin asks.

"A friend."

A few seconds pass before MINERVA replies from the WristTop. "*THE VEHICLE IS AHEAD 1.7 MILES. LEFT LANE.*"

"There it is," Franklin says. "The convertible."

Forceful air blows into the cab as Bragg rolls down the passenger side window. His blue tie flaps in the wind as he hangs his torso outside. He removes a ray gun from its holster and aims at the convertible. A squeeze of the trigger nearly sends the weapon flying from his grip as the blast jerks his arm upward. A brilliant red laser bolt sails through the air and grazes the back of the convertible.

Tough to wield, indeed.

As Bragg fires a few more rounds at the convertible, a silver hover van pulls in between and blocks his shot. The van is designed for families, complete with sliding side doors and a handy roof rack.

Bragg reenters the hatchback's passenger cab and reloads his ray guns with ammunition clips from his inner jacket pocket.

Ahead, the rear doors of the silver van fly open and reveal a young girl in an orange hoodie. She sits behind a built-in gatling gun. The barrel begins to spin and red laser bolts erupt from it at a dizzying rate, buzzing past the hatchback.

Franklin swerves to avoid the oncoming. Traffic in the street honk their horns and veer out of their path. Franklin screams with frustration and mashes the accelerator hard, pulling the hatchback alongside the hover van.

"Stay beside them!" Bragg yells to Franklin. Once his guns are reloaded, Bragg crawls partly outside the window again and holds on to the frame of the hatchback with his left hand.

Bragg removes a ray gun and squeezes the trigger repeatedly, producing a deafening sound. He starts to get a feel for the powerful weapons. Laser bolts erupt from the muzzle at a rapid pace, riddling the side of the van until it bursts into flames.

Franklin continues after the Asteroids, now fleeing across the Troxel Bridge.

Once Bragg spots them again he resumes his fire, striking the convertible until it starts to wobble on its axis. The vehicle weaves to the right and crashes into a lamp post with a thunderous pop. The front end caves in, sending debris sailing high into the air.

Franklin skids the hatchback to a halt in the middle of the eight-lane bridge.

Bragg and Franklin exit, sprinting toward the convertible. Bragg draws both his ray guns and approaches.

The airbag failed to deploy. The burly driver's head is a bloody mess, cracked open over the steering wheel. The skinny passenger is moaning and mumbling nonsense. The left part of his body is badly burned. His nose is broken, spilling blood down onto his orange coat.

"I'll deal with him," Bragg tells Franklin.

Bragg holsters his weapons. He grabs the Asteroid around the collar and lifts him out of the passenger seat with little effort. Bragg carries him to the side of the bridge and holds him over the edge.

The Asteroid begins to fidget, feet dangling like soft noodles.

The rage Bragg sensed earlier is growing worse.

"You . . . You can't kill me. It will start a war," the Asteroid says, between grunts.

A news chopper hovers above, shining a spotlight down onto the bridge. Bragg uses one hand to shield his eyes while looking up at it.

This causes the Asteroid to panic, grasping at Bragg even though his grip has not lessened.

Wherever I go, violence finds me.

"Let's leave before Enforcers get here!" Franklin yells.

"Where is your base?" Bragg asks the Asteroid.

"Our base? Who calls it that? Fuck you!" the Asteroid spouts, still flailing his legs.

Before he gives it much thought, Bragg releases his grip. Even as he watches the body fall, Bragg doesn't regret the decision. There is no splash, likely blanketed in the fog below.

Bragg waits until he is satisfied the Asteroid has drowned in the canal. He takes another look up at the news chopper and then sprints to the hatchback. He hops into the passenger seat.

Franklin speeds away.

After losing the news chopper, Franklin and Bragg return to the diner. They find the elderly couple crying and hugging each other in the corner booth.

"They've been dealt with," Franklin reports, as he and Bragg sit down across from the two.

"Thank you for standing up to those Asteroids," the man says. "Glad someone will. They claim to protect everyone, but they will hurt you and destroy things if you can't pay."

"Maybe these 'Asteroids' will leave you alone now," Bragg says.

"I doubt it," the woman replies. The nonchalance of her answer is cold and full of resentment.

"When do you think these Asteroids will return?" asks Bragg.

"I have no idea."

"What are your names?" he asks them.

"I'm Bryan and this is my wife Keisha," the man says. "This is our diner."

"How long has this been happening?"

"For the last few months."

"The Villains will provide protection from now on. We ask for nothing in return," Franklin interjects. "I'll send some guys down today."

The couple pepper Franklin and Bragg with gratitude. As they leave the diner, the owners wave at them, thanking them immensely.

Bragg is balancing four heavy bags of food in his arms, gifted from Bryan and Keisha. "Thank you for offering to help them."

"The people of Meridian need someone to stand up for them. Besides, I know you would have tried to help that couple, with or without our help," Franklin replies.

"My parents, before they died, taught me to stand up for those who can't stand up for themselves."

"I'm sorry to hear they are no longer with us. Would you mind if I asked how they passed?"

"My father died in a factory accident. My mother fell ill."

Bragg has not thought of his father for a long time; a strict man ripped from his life at age ten. Factory accidents like the one that claimed Paul Bragg would eventually result in tougher safety regulations. Paul's only son finds peace in the fact that his father's death resulted in changes that saved countless other sons from single-parent upbringings. However, deep down, Bragg is still that ten-year-old boy getting the news his father won't be coming home from work.

"Well, they taught you a wise lesson," Franklin says.

Bragg and Franklin return to the mansion. As they enter the kitchen, Bragg sets the bags on the marble island.

The gang starts to gather around, making their way to the food.

"Lunch is on Bragg today. He did good," Franklin announces to everyone. "After you eat, I need a couple of you to go down to the diner on Highland Street. Look after the older couple that owns it."

Bragg receives a few mumbled thanks and pats on the back from the very individuals responsible for his bruised ribs. Some compliment his new attire, which he enjoys more than he wants to admit. A few of them flash a hand sign, forming a "V" with their middle and ring finger.

Bragg returns the sign and follows Franklin upstairs to his study.

Inside, Franklin continues to orient Bragg. "Normally, a new recruit such as yourself would start small. Wearing the initiation jumpsuit. Transporting working girls. Corner hand to hands. However . . ."

The study door slams open, interrupting Franklin.

In walk Dawn and The Queen. Before anyone can say a word, The Queen blurts out: "These Asteroids hide out in a Comet City nightclub."

Dawn stands behind The Queen with a blank stare. Blood stains her blue sweater. She glances at Bragg, then abruptly exits the study holding her hand to her mouth.

Bragg pursues Dawn down the staircase and through the sprawling mansion. Eventually he catches up to her in one of the bathrooms, hunched over the toilet. Her face is pasty and her eyes are wide.

"You shouldn't care for someone like me. I'm no good," Dawn says as she flushes the toilet. Her sobs grow heavy and her body shakes. Tears run mascara down her cheeks.

Bragg looks around outside the bathroom, ensuring they are alone, and then closes the door behind him. "What happened?"

"The Queen told me the Asteroids took dancers from The Office and were using them . . . using them . . ." A violent spell of nausea pauses her words and she returns her face to the toilet bowl.

In a moment she wipes her mouth, takes a breath, and continues. "I told The Queen we had to get them back. She agreed, but took me behind the club and made me ki . . . she said she would kill . . . that I had to. . . I had to . . ." Dawn breaks out weeping.

She doesn't have to say it for Bragg to realize what has taken place.

Kill or be killed.

He squats down and embraces Dawn. She sobs so hard it sounds painful. This is an experience he can relate to. Taking life is existential. Feeling a person go from being to not-being is trauma no person can prepare for.

Bragg holds Dawn tighter. "You did what you had to. You're still here."

"Do you ever feel better about it?" Dawn asks, sniffing.

"No. But you learn to live with it."

They both grow quiet, clinging to each other. It seems his comment has calmed her a bit, but Bragg struggles to find more to say.

"I meant what I said. I know what you think you want with me. But everyone close to me gets hurt," Dawn says. "I'm not a monogamous kind of person, you know? Sex to me is . . . transactional."

"I got the impression it was something like that," Bragg says.

"I'm . . . really fucked up. You are not my type."

"What about Europa?" Bragg starts to feel uncomfortable. Sweating, he suddenly fears being without her.

"Some things are so arduous, they might as well be myth," she replies.

"I think I may . . ." Bragg continues, struggling to form his flood of emotion into words.

"You're fucking lame, spaceboy! Do I have to be brutally honest with you?" Dawn pushes Bragg away. "I don't fuck Union lackeys."

Before Bragg can say another word, The Queen knocks on the bathroom door and then speaks through it without waiting for an answer. "Dawn. Yer okay?"

Was she listening this entire time?

Dawn stands and snatches the door open. "Yeah."

"Then get where I need yer to be, bitch," The Queen snarls.

Something has changed. Bragg does not like it.

With a disappointed look on her face, Dawn crosses her arms and turns to Bragg. "Thank you for . . ." She leaves without finishing her thought.

The Queen steps into the bathroom and closes herself in with Bragg. Her muscular frame fills the small space. She opens her mouth and bares her sharp fangs. Bragg springs to his feet, concerned about his odds if things get hostile.

"If I ever see yer around Dawn again, yer better be paying credits fer it."

"Or what . . .?" Bragg asks.

"Listen, yer new so I'll cut yer some slack. Those wittle ray guns are hardly enough to stop me from fucking snapping yer in two," she warns.

Stubbornly, Bragg reaches into his suit jacket for his ray guns. Before he can get them unholstered, The Queen lunges toward Bragg and pins him against the bathroom wall. Her large hand grips his neck until oxygen struggles to reach his brain. He has never felt such helplessness.

When she lets him go, Bragg falls to the ground coughing. Tears fill his eyes to the point that he is blind. Once he recovers, The Queen has vanished.

It is an odd sensation to lose someone you never really had. As he sits beside the puke-reeking toilet, anguish weighs Bragg down. The Queen seems to be both an unstoppable force and an immovable object.

But a squad man never gives up.

-----

8. Hell
"Who's gonna stop us? Tis clown?"

Hell is the only reason most of the solar system has ever heard of The Asteroids. The nightclub's reputation has made it a must-see destination for occult tourists. Lore says the club was an old bunker from the First Interplanetary War, when it was used to execute prisoners by pushing them into a pit and onto spikes protruding up from the floor. Dawn figures the Asteroids made the story up themselves to draw bigger crowds.

But who knows?

The front of the night club is bustling. The outside is painted bright red with countless glowing skulls embedded into the wall. A long line of hopeful club goers congregate along the sidewalk, barricaded like cattle behind a velvet rope.

The women all look into WristTop mirrors, fixing excessive makeup or snapping selfies.

The men gawk at Dawn and The Queen as they skip the line, both clad in provocative black dresses and draped in mink.

The Queen's bravado worries Dawn. She struts and taunts everyone as she passes, mumbling insults under her breath. From their expressions, the crowd is upset at The Queen's behavior.

According to Bragg, tonight is just for something called *"re-con-nais-sance."* A few Villains are to sneak into Hell to see how many Asteroids are inside.

This course of action is unsatisfactory for The Queen. She has arrived early and forced Dawn to come along.

"This is not wise," Dawn says. She lags behind The Queen, covertly typing a message to Bragg on her WristTop.

The Queen is going to stir things up. "Fuck yer boyfriend's plan. The Villains need me. I don't need them. By the time they arrive, all the Asteroids will be dead."

Dawn and The Queen walk up to the entrance bouncer. An orange bandanna is tied around his wrist. When he notices Dawn and The Queen approaching, his eyes drop straight to their chests. A goofy grin reveals two buck front teeth.

"What are you going to do? We can't cut all these people in line," Dawn whispers to The Queen.

"Who's gonna stop us? Tis clown?" The Queen replies, pointing at the bouncer.

"Take it easy," Dawn pleads. She steps ahead of The Queen and captures the bouncer's gaze. Once she is close enough, Dawn gently takes his hand and smiles big. "I'm Tanya and this is Zu. We're with the DJ."

The bouncer steps back and opens the entrance without question. Dawn lets out a sigh of relief.

I can't believe that old trick worked.

Once they are beyond the bouncer's earshot, she leans over to The Queen. "We can't push our way in here. This is their club."

"I knew yer would come through. I mean who could resist yer?"

They turn the corner and enter the intense club. Smoke lingers in the air, giving the space a nightmarish vibe. There is a musty stench. Infernal decorations line the walls, painted with glow-in-the-dark flames that flicker. A steep concrete slope leads downward to a humongous pit full of people moshing around. Neo-techno music blares from overhead speakers.

A DJ booth hangs by chains above the massive mosh pit. The DJ is wearing a giant electronic skull head that glows bright red and pulsates with the rhythm of the music.

Also hanging above the pit are cages with girls dancing inside. They are completely nude, wearing only a collar around their necks.

Like animals.

Dawn tries to make out their faces, but the lighting is too poor.

The Queen's lips are moving, but Dawn cannot hear her. Dawn points above to the cages, trying to direct her attention to the girls. It's to no avail. Abruptly The Queen starts down the slope, toward the moshers.

Dawn follows her, struggling to keep up. Sweaty dancers bump into Dawn and push her around. All of them are dressed in black with blank faces. Everyone appears to be high. The atmosphere feels more cult-like than party. She feels stuck in place, suffocated by the mass of bodies surrounding her.

Ahead she can see The Queen moving farther and farther away, pushing herself a path through the moshers.

Suddenly the music cuts out and is replaced with a blood-curdling roar. The crowd calms as all the lights flicker bright red and turn on and off in a way that would doom an epileptic.

Subtle tingles make their way up Dawn's back.

I wish I was high.

A gigantic demonic figure materializes above the mosh pit out of thin air. The hologram is a vivid, muscular human male, completely nude with glowing red skin. Black horns protrude from his forehead.

Its realism leaves Dawn simultaneously wanting to run away and unable to move.

The demon rides around above the crowd on a fiery steed. When the demon lets out a grim laugh, the beat of the music drops again and the pit starts moshing harder than before.

Dawn shoves through the crowd, looking for a way to get to the cages hanging above.

A broad-shouldered man steps into her path, cutting her off. He is wearing an orange short-sleeve collared shirt. His face is stern.

Dawn tries to resist, pushing him in the chest with both arms extended – but she is no match.

He bear-hugs Dawn, picking her up and throwing her over his shoulder. The man carries Dawn up a set of stairs in the back of the club. On the way up, Dawn has a straight view of the hanging cages. This time she notices Crystal and Imani. The girls look exhausted and barely recognizable.

They enter an office overlooking the mosh pit. Inside, elegance and sophistication replace the dopamine binge occurring downstairs. Marble floors complement a grand oak desk. Sitting before it are two matching oak chairs. Dawn's body stings as the man throws her to the floor and then leaves.

A dark-skinned male swivels around in a chair behind the desk. He is overweight but well groomed. His hair is neatly cut, as well as his goatee. A tailored black suit compliments his orange vest and tie.

"Dawn is your true name, isn't it?" he says. His voice is silky and smooth.

Dawn can sense he is dangerous. Even though she is nervous, Dawn attempts to play it cool. "We want our dancers back. The ones you took from The Office and forced to dance here," Dawn says, as she stands up.

"Forced? We forced them no more than Franklin did. You should understand that."

"The Villains don't force workers to do anything," Dawn protests, half-heartedly.

"Then why haven't you left? You like pleasing others so much that you will hand over the credits you earn to Franklin Hendrix?"

She ignores the Asteroid's valid point. "Give us the dancers and we will leave."

"What about a trade? I hear you are a far better dancer than all of them combined." The Asteroid rises from his chair. He grins, revealing his deep dimples. He waddles to the front of his desk and leans back against it. "Let's see it."

Dawn glances behind her, at the closed office door. She worries about the Asteroid's reaction should she decline his offer.

The male ego is fragile.

Shrugging her shoulders, Dawn lets her blue mink drop to the floor. She bites her lip seductively. "Do you have any music? Other than this rave shit?"

The Asteroid reaches down and presses a few buttons on his WristTop. The sound from outside the office is blocked out, replaced by a sultry song.

Dawn places both her hands on her breasts, massaging them through her black dress. She stares into the Asteroid's eyes from across the room. Slowly making her way towards him, swaying her hips to the melody of the song.

Once she is close enough, Dawn reaches a hand out and caresses his chubby cheek. He releases an audible sigh as she touches his skin. His eyes get droopy. "What is your name handsome?"

"Aster . . ." the man mumbles.

Dawn feels around the desk behind Aster. Her hand finds a drinking glass, heavy enough to accomplish her goal. She leans in to kiss Aster, while also lifting the glass behind his head.

Suddenly the glint of laser rounds flash outside the office window.

Aster also notices the red and green flickers. He pushes his WristTop again, stopping the sultry music. "What the fuck?"

Dawn and Aster walk over to the window. Below she can see the Villains flooding into the club. Bragg is in front, wielding twin ray guns. Orange-clad men and women are weaving through the dark crowd of moshers, engaging in the firefight.

Despite the laser rounds, the moshers continue to thrash about to the blaring music. Dawn can't tell if they think this is all part of the act or they just don't care. The deadly lightshow flickers around them, collecting more and more innocents the longer it persists.

With Aster distracted, Dawn bashes him over the head with the glass. He falls to the ground, moaning, before passing out.

Dawn freezes. Her mind says 'go' but her body will not obey. Fear has locked her in place, turning her into a statute. She looks out to the cages. Her co-workers look terrified, trapped above the mayhem.

There is narrow scaffolding above the cages. *Staying still will be my demise.*

Dawn grabs one of the oak chairs from in front of the desk. It is almost too heavy for her to handle, but that is a good thing. She charges the office window, chair extended in front of her. It breaks the glass and rains shards down onto the moshers below.

Without giving herself time to reconsider, Dawn follows the chair out the window. She accesses the scaffolding and starts to crawl across the thin metal. Thousands of laser rounds echo through the reverberating music below. Dawn keeps her eyes forward, not daring to look down. She can see a panel about ten yards ahead.

Once Dawn reaches the panel, she observes buttons with arrows pointing up, down and side to side. She mashes the button with the up arrow and the scaffolding starts to shudder. A pulley system of chains that hang from the ceiling rattle to life around her.

The cages are raised until they are lined up next to the scaffolding path Dawn just crossed. Their metal doors spring open. Crystal, Imani and Destiny are freed. All three are only wearing a thick black collar with a loop in the front for a leash. They hug Dawn as if they are long-lost friends.

"I can't believe it's you!" Imani shouts over the noise. Naturally pretty, Imani is a bit of a tomboy, with corn rolled hair and an aversion to cosmetics. Dark bags sag under her eyes. "I thought we were going to die in those cages. They haven't given us any food or water."

Although they all express tremendous gratitude, Dawn wonders how many of them would have done the same were the roles reversed.

"We have to get out of here," Crystal says. She has red hair and a slight gap in her front teeth. "I'm ready to go home."

Then a deep, demonic voice speaks from everywhere. "*Disciples . . . onslaught!*"

The music changes again, this time to a fast tempo metal song. The moshers begin to attack the Villains in the pit below. They lunge and claw like rabid animals. Even laser rounds fail to stop the moshers. Now with an army of drugged-up zombies, the Asteroids overwhelm the Villains.

Bragg!

Dawn sees The Queen climbing the hanging DJ booth, a long slit ripped in her dress. The DJ's glowing red skull turns and looks at The Queen once she pulls herself over the side. The Queen signals with her hands for the DJ to turn off the music.

Paying her no attention, the DJ turns back to his control board.

The Queen then punches the DJ hard in the side, causing him to double over. She begins pulling wires from the control board until the music suddenly stops.

The moshers stop their assault and send up disapproving boos up to the DJ booth. They seem unaware they just attacked the Villains. Their faces are blank again.

The Queen snatches up the DJ and throws him from the booth, down into the pit. His body hits the cement with a resounding thud.

A brief silence overtakes the crowd before the moshers stampede towards the exit.

The firefight between the Villains and Asteroids resumes.

Dawn and the freed dancers hide in the rafters above the club as the establishment lives up to its name. No matter how firmly she holds her hands to her ears, the chaotic noise invades. No matter how much of a ball she squeezes her body into, she cannot escape into herself.

-----

9. Avenger
"Do yourself a favor and forget about Dawn."

A hover car, matte black in color, blasts through the streets of Meridian. The retracted convertible roof allows the moon to paint the leather seats with a soft glow. The Doctor is behind the wheel, a wry smile raising his cheekbones as he weaves the car in and out of traffic. He is wearing an untucked royal blue dress shirt. His loose black tie is whipping in the wind over his shoulder.

Bragg sits in the passenger seat, regretting his decision to allow Zin to drive. "It'd be wise to slow down, with us being wanted fugitives and all," Bragg says.

"Don't tell me how to drive," Zin replies. "This is a turbo. It's meant to go fast."

Bragg dislikes the Doctor. Every second spent with him is taxing. "Where are we going?"

"Franklin thinks you're some master tactician since you helped take out the Asteroids."

"I'm not."

"Trust me, I don't think you are either," Zin says. "Nonetheless, Franklin wants me to babysit you. We are going to my place. Might as well crash there."

Zin pulls the hover car into the parking garage of a high-rise apartment building. They get out and get into an elevator, which takes them to the penthouse level. The doors open to a brilliant open layout.

Tall windows surround the space. Meridian's skyline decorates the backdrop with skyscrapers illuminated in checkered patterns. The floor is white marble. The furniture is black leather.

"This is . . . nice," Bragg admits.

"Thanks," the Doctor replies.

Odd. No snappy comeback.

"You can crash in the spare bedroom," Zin adds.

"Thanks," Bragg replies.

"Just keep pulling your weight and we are good." Zin walks to the kitchen and grabs a beer from the refrigerator.

"Are you really a doctor?" Bragg takes a seat on the couch.

"Naw. My asshole dad just always wanted me to go to medical school. I took the name to spite him. He is a wealthy mineral refiner on Mars. My mom is a failed model, who was more focused on her career than raising my older sister and me. I dropped out of private school during twelfth year and joined the

Villains. I can care less about the Alpha family name. I am going to become the most infamous gangster in the solar system."

A chime sounds from Zin's WristTop. He presses a button and Franklin's face appears on the screen.

"Get down to the diner soon as you can," Franklin says.

"It's 1:00 a.m. It can't wait?" the Doctor groans.

"No. Bring Bragg with you." Franklin's face disappears from the screen.

"Well 'Doc,' time to pull our weight," Bragg says.

The duo loads back into the convertible and heads to the diner. The night air gently roars up the windshield and over Bragg's head. He leans back and stares up into the sky, as streetlights and overpasses dart by.

"You're thinking of her aren't you?" Zin asks Bragg.

He is right.

Not a day goes by without Bragg thinking of Dawn. Some days it's a little, others it's a lot. Since their last conversation, he has sent a message to her WristTop every morning. He checks for a reply constantly throughout the day, hoping it will be different from the day prior.

It never is.

Bragg remains silent, which is confirmation enough for Zin. "I hate to say I told you so."

"I'm not sure that's true," Bragg replies.

"Some girls are not worth it. Do yourself a favor and forget about Dawn."

Zin pulls the convertible over to the curb, bringing it to a stop in front of Bryan and Keisha's diner. He continues his advice as if he truly were a doctor, licensed in counseling. "If you really want closure? Go down to The Office, find the sexiest dancer and get the nastiest lap dance imaginable – all where Dawn can see."

Inside, they find Bryan hunched over in the kitchen behind the counter. His wife, Keisha, wipes down the counter while wearing a disposable plastic apron and yellow rubber gloves.

"Hello, Doc. Bragg." Keisha greets them before returning her attention to the counter.

Bragg glances at Franklin, sitting in the corner booth wearing a crisp white dress shirt. Next to him sits someone petite and hidden in an oversized black hoodie. "Bragg! Zin!" calls Franklin. "Come and join me."

They both take a seat. Keisha brings them a thermos of coffee and two more cups.

"Is the Doctor looking after you?" Franklin asks, pouring them each a cup of coffee.

"Yes," Bragg replies, nodding at Zin.

"Did he tell you about the Governor's Ball?"

"I was going to tell him . . ." Zin answers, shrugging at Bragg.

"It's in a few days, at the mansion. Some of the most powerful people in the solar system will be in attendance. Have Howard get you a tuxedo."

Doesn't sound like my kind of party.

"And . . . I must attend?" Bragg asks hesitantly, so as not to offend.

"Of course! You are the man of the hour," Franklin says. "The Asteroids are a thing of the past, thanks to you."

"It took effort from the entire gang to end the Rocks – " the Doctor interjects.

"And I've heard there are still a few left," Bragg adds.

"Speaking of that," Franklin says, finally motioning to the person sitting next to him. "This is Kora, one of our best working girls. She caught a rough date earlier."

"Caught a rough date?" Bragg asks.

Franklin motions to Kora. "Show them, sweetheart. It's okay."

The hood falls back, revealing a young face brutally scarred with fresh laser knife wounds. The burns are slashed diagonally from her temple to her chin, in crisscross fashion. Kora has long dark hair and huge hazel eyes that are clouded with sadness.

Zin flinches at the sight of her, causing the girl to sob.

"Who did this to you?" Bragg asks softly.

There is no answer. Only tears.

"She hasn't talked. But she has agreed to take us to where she caught the date. And to point out the person responsible," Franklin says. "I need someone with the stomach to make this right, if you understand."

Tension builds in Bragg's neck and shoulders. Even though things are getting ludicrous, he cannot bring himself to walk away. Deep down, he is enjoying life with the Villains. He wants nothing more than to help Kora bring revenge to her assailant. He longs for another good fight.

"When did this happen to her?" Bragg asks.

"As far as we know, a few hours ago," Franklin replies.

"Come with us, Kora. We need your help just for a little. Then you can rest," Bragg states.

Kora wipes her eyes and nods without looking up. She follows Bragg and the Doctor outside to the convertible. She is wearing dingy grey shorts. Most of the skin on her scrawny, sun-kissed legs is reddened with deep lacerations.

Beneath her new facial scars, Bragg can tell Kora is pretty. He does not think she is any less so with the burns, but doubts she can be convinced of that any time soon.

Kora rides in the back seat, providing directions with her finger. She leads Bragg and Zin to a run-down hostel. The outside is deteriorated brick and overgrown shrubbery. The structure is narrow. There are stairs leading from the sidewalk up through the middle of the building. Doors leading to *pay per hour* rooms line both sides.

Five individuals linger at the foot of the stairwell, idly chatting and cracking jokes on the sidewalk. They are drinking heavily and becoming more and more intoxicated.

Bragg and Zin sit with Kora in the convertible, hidden from view behind an automated food truck.

"No telling how many people are in there. No proof the person that fucked up her face is even here either," Doc protests.

"He's in there." Kora finally speaks. "Top of the stairs, on the left." Her voice is more mature than her appearance.

Bragg peers into the back seat. Kora is no longer looking down. She glares at the hostel. Rage fills her face.

Bragg matches her energy.

"We need more Villains. We can't just go barging in like we are The Queen," Zin says.

The Queen. Hearing her name sets Bragg off. Coupled with the vengeful look in Kora's eyes, he can take it no more.

In one motion, Bragg is out of the hover car. "If you don't like it, Doc, stay out of the way." Bragg stops at the trunk of the convertible and removes as many extra rounds as he can fit into his suit jacket.

Without coaxing, Kora exits the vehicle as well, tagging along behind Bragg as he crosses the street toward the hostel. Her vulnerable demeanor has evaporated.

The individuals outside the hostel are so inebriated they fail to notice Bragg until he is right upon them.

Their first mistake.

The first man eats his teeth before he has time to warn the others. Two more are incapacitated by more of Bragg's violent punches.

Kora screams, brandishing a laser pistol and finishing the rest.

Bragg is astonished at her decent accuracy.

I wish she would have held off, though.

From the foot of the steep stairs, Bragg stares upward as doors on both sides fly open.

Orange-clad goons flood out, armed with hand cannons.

Bragg grabs Kora and pulls her into cover behind a hover car parked at the curb.

The goons open fire. The air is filled with the stinging, reverberating sound of laser rounds as they riddle the car.

Eventually, the rounds cease. Bragg peeks around the back of the hover car and sees that the Asteroid goons are almost upon them. He removes his twin ray guns, bracing himself to take out as many as he can.

Zin appears from what seems like thin air, returning fire with a laser pistol and dropping enough of the orange-clad individuals to make the rest hesitate to advance. They retreat up the stairs and disappear into the doorways of the rental rooms.

"What now, genius?" Zin yells, as he joins them behind the hover car.

Bragg peaks around the car again, counting at least seven deceased Asteroids laid out on the sidewalk. There can't be many left. He raises his WristTop to his mouth. "MINERVA. Are you around?"

"IN THE CLOUDS ABOVE YOU, COMMANDER."

"I need a thermal scan of this hostel behind me."

"Who are you talking to?" Zin asks.

Bragg ignores the Doctor. He studies the scans made by the Mark IX, displayed on his WristTop as yellow and red patches of color. "Come on. There are only a few remaining."

Bragg sprints from behind the car and races up the stairwell. He kicks into one of the hostel rooms, shooting the two surviving Asteroids he finds. Bragg then uses the doorway as cover as he fires his ray guns up the steps at the other goons.

Zin and Kora follow his lead, clearing the area until they make it to the top of the stairs. They stand before the final room. Kora kicks the door so hard it startles Bragg. She is strong for having such a short stature. The door takes two more kicks before falling from its hinges.

Whimpering on the ground is a sweaty, balding man dressed in nothing but an open orange robe.

"This guy had plenty of time to put on some pants," Zin quips.

Bragg wastes no time. "Why did you scar her face?"

It takes a few malice-fueled punches to extract a confession.

"I wanted the girl to work for me. When she refused, I took a laser knife to her face," the balding man admits.

"Who are you?" Zin asks.

"I'm . . . I'm Stephan. I took over the Asteroids after Aster."

"Never heard of you. And we killed all the Rocks," Zin says.

Kora pushes past Bragg and begins to press her thumbs into Stephan's eye sockets. He lets out horrible screams. Blood streams from his face.

"You enjoy inflicting pain? I'll show you pain, you sick fuck!" The eye jabs were her kindest gestures. Once she removes a laser knife from her front hoodie pocket, things get even worse.

Halfway through Kora's ten minutes of torturing Stephan, Bragg realizes her viciousness exceeds anyone he has ever known. Even those twisted by war.

Then again, those face wounds couldn't have happened quickly.

Kora was a prisoner of war. A victim returned to get retribution on her predator.

When she is done, Kora drops her laser knife and wanders past Bragg with a dazed look. Under her breath, so quietly Bragg almost misses it, Kora says, "Thank you."

-----

10. Plots and Plans
"The Queen does not own you."

Life comes full circle.

The Office has reopened. Franklin has made Dawn manager of the vibrant establishment. She stands on the new balcony, overlooking the renovated club. Music reverberates off the walls. Downstairs, naked women and men dance on stage entertaining rowdy patrons.

Residents of Meridian treat the Villains like celebrities. Members of the gang stand at the bar, posing for pictures and signing autographs. Every night is like this. The Office has become one of the most popular clubs in the region. The place is filled to capacity with horny Union citizens and dissidents. The waitresses keep the drinks flowing as people spend away their savings and ill-gotten gains.

Despite The Office's success, Dawn cannot shake a chronic sense of dejection.

Something is missing.

Lately, The Queen has gloated over Dawn with a mixture of affection and infliction.

Gifts one moment, belittling tirades another. The dramatic swing in emotion is exhausting.

Raging jealousy spurs The Queen. Even though Dawn strives to hide her feelings, it's as if The Queen can smell it on her. She constantly demands to know Dawn's location and scares off anyone who dares flirt with her.

Dawn has been inadvertently granted a short reprieve. Franklin has sent The Queen west of the continent to do something secret. Freedom from her constant, ever watchful eye has been refreshing.

As she makes her way down the stairs, Dawn tugs the bottom of her short black cocktail dress. She mingles, visiting with patrons and checking on staff. In a private booth, she spots Zin. He appears drunk with his arms wrapped around a green-skinned alien dancer.

Dawn hoped to see Bragg with Zin, but no such luck. Bragg does not visit The Office.

Not anymore.

"I'm glad to see you showing the rest of the gang how to have a good time," Dawn shouts to Zin.

"Dawn! I'm here to support your business. That's all," he replies, laughing.

Dawn exits the club and stands on the sidewalk outside. The weather is brisk. A line extends from the door, comprised of people enduring the frigid weather to access what lies inside. Dawn's long overcoat sways with the breeze as she awaits the hover car scheduled to escort her.

Surely, Bragg will be at the Ball.

Despite its prestigious name, the Governor's Ball is just an excuse for corrupt politicians to party with their seedier constituents. It is a safe, controlled setting to play gangster with gangsters. Working girls mark the date of the Ball on their calendar. It's an opportunity to make a year's worth of credits in one night; more if you're willing to be as entertaining as the politicians usually want you to be.

A hoverbike pulls over to the curb before Dawn. Bragg is atop it.

Dawn's heart stops.

Bragg gets off the bike and stands at attention. He is wearing a fitted black tuxedo and bow tie.

He is . . . grittier.

Everything Dawn expected to feel when she saw Bragg again is ten times more intense. It is difficult to conceal. As she walks over to greet him, Dawn leans in to hug Bragg.

Initially he returns the gesture, before jerking to a stop and extending a handshake.

Of course.

She accepts his handshake.

"How have you been?" he asks.

"Good. Glad you finally came to check out the new club. I owe you a dance."

His face flinches at the thought, then retreats into bashfulness. "Did you get – ? I – I sent some – " he stutters.

She had. Daily WristTop messages checking in on her. Dawn deleted them all to hide them from The Queen. "Yes. I'm sorry . . ." she starts, unable to explain her unresponsiveness.

"It's fine. Where is The Queen?"

"West coast, on business."

"I see," Bragg replies. "Well, I've got a surprise for you." Bragg motions to the hoverbike behind him.

"You bought this?"

"Yes. For you."

Dawn runs the tips of her fingers along the sleek black paint. She circles the bike with admiration, jaw agape. It is slimmer than her prior model. The bike is bulky in the front with a stubby, horizontal wing on the bottom. The back curves upward into a narrow seat for a passenger.

"Why would you do this?" Dawn asks.

"The hoverbike you had when we met is in the Enforcer impound. This was easier than getting it out," Bragg replies.

"Bragg . . . I . . ." Dawn stammers. She walks over to Bragg and kisses him.

Kissing Bragg is different. His quivering lips divulge his inexperience.

Her faint gasp reveals her genuine passion. Dawn comes to her senses and slightly shoves Bragg away. "This must have cost a fortune."

"Doc and I have been doing pretty well. And I don't need much to get by."

"I don't mean to sound ungrateful, but you shouldn't buy me things."

"Why? Because of The Queen? She doesn't scare me."

"No. Because it's dumb to buy stuff for a working girl. And The Queen should scare you."

"I'm repaying a debt. You lost your hoverbike helping me."

"Well . . . do you want to take me for a ride?" Dawn asks.

Bragg reaches into his inner suit pocket, pulls out a blocky key, and tosses it to Dawn. "It's your bike. You will have to take me for a ride."

Even though she is wearing the short cocktail dress beneath her coat, Dawn hikes it up and straddles her new bike.

Bragg climbs on the back and places his arm around her waist.

A smile stretches Dawn's face.

I have missed him.

They spend the evening adventuring around Meridian. Dawn is overcome with joy.

She resembles her old self, changing the station on the radio and singing along to the melodies.

Dawn pulls the hoverbike over at Haven's Hill, a cemetery overlooking the sea of lights from downtown Meridian.

Bragg gets off the bike to stretch his legs, taking in the view.

Dawn sits on the hoverbike, taking puffs of a cannabis e-cigarette.

Bragg turns and stares at her with a serious look.

"Are you judging me?" Dawn asks.

"No. It's just . . ."

"Here. Try it." She walks over and places the e-cigarette in Bragg's inner suit pocket.

"I've been thinking about how to get to Europa," Bragg says.

"It's not that I don't want to run away with you Bragg. The Queen won't let us go. She will kill you if you keep pursuing me. She is obsessed." A wave of emotion overcomes Dawn and she places another passionate kiss on his lips. She almost feels she means it.

"The Queen doesn't own you."

"No, she does not. But it's complicated. The Queen isn't all bad. I've known her since I was sixteen. After splitting with my third pimp, I took a shuttle from Musk to Meridian. The Queen approached me at the shuttle station. She promised to have the solution to all my problems.

"Right away she introduced me to Franklin and the Villains, and I began working as a waitress at The Office. Although The Queen was frightening to the rest of the gang, she was always nice to me – in the beginning.

"She told me her life story, too. At age seven, her parents loaded her onto a ship with three other children and sent them on a one-way trip to Earth. Their efforts were a desperate attempt to preserve their race from a war-torn planet.

"At the time, I found Shea's story relatable. I also knew what it was like to be torn from biological parents at a young age… and I've always found Shea attractive. That's where most of the problem lies. Shea and I fell in love. We were inseparable for about a year. But she's the reason why I'm stuck in this life."

"A life of dancing on tables at The Office," said Bragg.

"Yeah… and worse. Once we were dating, The Queen introduced me to narcotics. Meteor dust, mainly. She would encourage it, supplying me with everything I could possibly want – until she didn't. Once addiction dug its claws in, The Queen refused to keep supplying the narcotics. Instead, she made me work for my fix.

"At first, it was just exotic dancing. The tips were terrible and by the end of the night I owed more than I made for the narcotics I consumed during my shift. That's when The Queen convinced me to become a working girl and provide more than lap dances to the club's more invested customers. It was all based on manipulation. Most of the other working girls admitted that The Queen lured them into the lifestyle the same way she lured me."

"Well, you don't owe her anything. And she won't kill me," Bragg says. He grabs Dawn's hand.

There is something about his grip, and the sharp look in his grey eyes, that makes Dawn believe him.

-----

11. The Governor's Ball
"Are you with me now?"

Bragg and Dawn arrive at the mansion to find it bustling with activity. The Governor's Ball is well underway. Villains are posted around the perimeter. Hover cars pack the driveway, forcing the duo to park Dawn's new bike on the street.

Dawn is next to Bragg as they walk up the driveway. She is wearing a long blue overcoat and a short black cocktail dress beneath. Her heels have lacy straps that crisscross up to her mid shin. Her purple hair is straightened.

She looks great.

Inside, the entire foyer has been converted into a dance floor. Techno hip hop is blaring. The acoustics, combined with the makeshift lighting, create an electric vibe. The attendees are all wearing formal attire. They dance and sing, with a cup either held to their lips or up in the air.

Dawn splits from Bragg and joins the party.

The trek up the stairs annoys Bragg. An endless stream of belligerent fools stand in his way. It's odd to see people who appear on the news services, usually debating policies and assuring everyone the solar system is safe, plastered with alcohol in a gang's hideout. These are politicians slumming it on Earth, doing things that would end their careers if made public.

Bragg enters Franklin's study and finds him staring at the fireplace, holding a glass of alcohol. He is wearing a three-piece tuxedo with a royal blue tie. His dreads are tied neatly in a bun atop his head. Bragg closes the door behind him.

"It's a madhouse downstairs. Most of the Villains are drunk," Bragg informs him.

"It's a party, my boy. You still have so much Space Force training in you. Relax," Franklin says.

Bragg grows cautious.

I'm no boy.

Franklin stares into his drink in silence for a moment before taking a swig. "When I met you, I knew you had potential, but I had no idea how much. A while back, I met another with potential. That was Shea Shibaz, The Queen. She had run away from an orphanage. I thought I could help her – groom her to take my place as this gang's leader. However, I am certain now that she is far too rough around the edges to lead." Franklin gulps down the rest of his drink.

"But I think maybe you could. The gang respects you."

Bragg is hesitant to say anything. A couple of months ago, he was wandering the streets of Meridian. Now, not only is he a member of a space gang, the leader is asking him to someday take his place.

Time flies.

Although the idea is somewhat appealing, Bragg does not like the sound of being 'groomed.'

"While I am grateful for your faith in me, surely there are members of the Villains that have been loyal. And who have been around a lot longer than me," Bragg says.

"Longevity does not necessarily make one fit to lead," Franklin counters.

Bragg nods in agreement to his point, but says nothing more.

Franklin makes another drink from a drink cart in the corner, apparently agreeing to drop the subject for now. "I hear the last of the Asteroids are gone," he says.

"Yes. The Doctor and I made sure of it," Bragg replies.

Franklin chuckles and gulps the second drink. "Well, go downstairs and enjoy the Ball."

"But . . ."

"Relax, Bragg. I'm serious," Franklin says.

Urged out of the study, Bragg returns to the Ball. He removes Dawn's cannabis e-cigarette from his inner jacket pocket and puffs it. After a few violent coughs, he tries it again.

As he stands overlooking the foyer, Bragg spots Dawn dancing in the crowd below. Her purple hair bounces around her head as she jigs. She is surrounded by working girls, all doing the same. Bragg looks on, watching Dawn enjoy herself. Sweat blankets her toned body in a way that appeals to him.

He makes his way down the stairs and through the crowd as if no one else is present. Bragg starts to loosen up, continuing to puff the cigarette. His body feels weightless. His brain is fuzzy.

Each face he passes is ecstatic. The Villains praise Bragg, shaking his hand and patting him on the back. The sense of *belonging* has cured his depression.

His surroundings morph into a tunnel. Sound garbles. All Bragg can see is Dawn's beauteousness.

When Dawn notices Bragg a few feet away, she shoos the other working girls away.

"I didn't mean to interrupt," Bragg says, just loud enough to be heard over the music.

"You're just who I wanted to see," she replies.

The music's volume dies down. Franklin stands above the crowd, at the top of the staircase. He clips on a lapel microphone, which amplifies his voice. Everyone in the foyer turns their attention towards him, including Dawn and Bragg.

"I don't mean to interrupt the celebration, but I did want to thank everyone for attending the seventh annual Governor's Ball!"

The crowd claps in unison, forcing Franklin to pause. He looks gracious but unamused as he waits for the applause to subside. "I'd also like to mention a few things," he says.

Looking around, Bragg notices every single person appears to be awaiting Franklin's next words. Although most of them are drunk or high, they all show the leader tremendous respect.

Politicians and Villains.

"We have been put in tough spots time and time again, yet we find a way to pull it out. The Asteroids put us in the toughest of spots. Now they are no more!"

A short burst of cheers and shouts follow Franklin's increasing enthusiasm.

Bragg passes the cannabis e-cigarette to Dawn.

She grins and takes it from him.

"While I'm proud of our recent success, I cannot take all the credit. It was a well-executed

plan by our commander, Samuel Bragg,"
Franklin continues.

Bragg's jaw drops to the floor. Anxiety
smashes into him like a pane of glass.

Franklin waves Bragg up towards him,
inviting him to speak.

Is this some kind of test?

Bragg feels like he is back at the Space
Force Academy.

The politicians clap, looking around for
the master tactician whom Franklin is praising.

After hesitating for as long as he can,
Bragg ascends the stairs and stands next to
Franklin. A sea of eyes peer up at him from the
foyer. Their glares are intense and judging. He
can hear them thinking about what an imposter
he is.

*The plan didn't even work, thanks to The
Queen.*

Franklin unclips the mic from his lapel
and onto Bragg's.

Bragg regrets smoking cannabis. If
someone dropped anything, it could be heard
through the silent anticipation. He surveys the
faces before attempting the unimaginable.

"A lot of you don't know me. However, I
imagine we are all the same in a lot of ways," he
starts, pleased to have achieved most of the
captive audience Franklin had. "I grew up in the
slums. Never had much of anything. I left Earth

and joined the Space Force to see the solar system."

Aside from his voice, the entire mansion is deadly quiet. Bragg is unsure if that is a good sign or a bad sign. He pauses again, searching for the courage to push forward.

"The Union brainwashed me. So, I ran away. I was scared. Until I found the Villains."

A low but steady ballyhoo simmers in the crowd.

"A group that strives to be free of Union conditioning. That struggles to maintain freedom of choice. A choice that cowards in the shadows try to steal from us."

Villains shout in agreement.

"This gang has and will continue to accomplish enormous feats. We will defeat enemies and form alliances that will push Meridian into the new era!"

The room erupts with thunderous applause. The Villains lose it, tossing liquor into the air as they cheer.

Bragg can see the pride exuding from everyone as they high five and drunkenly cling to each other.

Franklin pats Bragg on the shoulder. "That is what makes one fit to lead."

Before Bragg can respond, Franklin goes down the stairs and disappears into the crowd of partying attendees.

As Bragg descends the stairs, the Villains cheer and toast him. Someone brings him a cup, which he gulps down without asking what is in it. The liquid is syrupy and sweet.

The music resumes and the Ball carries on.

Dawn approaches Bragg with a big smile. "Impressive."

"I was a commander, you know," Bragg replies.

"Sounds to me like you still are." Dawn pulls Bragg into the dancing crowd.

Villains bring Bragg drinks by the twos. Things grow more carefree. In the center of the massive crowd, Bragg and Dawn dance in their own bubble. Her tight body grinds against him, luring him in.

Today must be a dream.

Dawn takes her hand and places it on her belly button. Bragg watches as she playfully wiggles her fingers, running them up her sweat-drenched dress. She reaches into her bra, removes a red pill, and gently presses it to Bragg's lips, motioning for him to take it into his mouth.

Initially, Bragg resists. The pill could be anything. At worst, poison from some secret plot to kill him; at best, some narcotic he is allergic to.

"Trust me, handsome," Dawn murmurs.

Fuck, no.

Bragg stares back into Dawn's deep purple eyes. Her pupils and sclera are as brilliant as handcrafted marbles. He can hear his mind screaming *spit the pill on the floor!* but his drunken heart yells louder, telling him that he should venture out with this alluring vixen.

Bragg takes the pill onto his tongue and swallows it with a big gulp. As Bragg and Dawn continue to dance, the music grows increasingly vivid to his ears. Every note is more pleasing, showering them from above and bouncing off the walls.

The mansion's light show gives her model-like face different tints and hues. As Dawn moves, a swirling outline of her silhouette begins to follow her, tracking her body like a technicolor shadow.

Unsure if this is real, Bragg reaches out and touches Dawn's face with the tips of his fingers. This causes tiny sparks to exude from his fingernails. He cannot believe his eyes.

"Are you with me now?" Dawn asks.

Then she is gone.

The night feels like it is never ending. Bragg continues to drink, sharing cannabis cigarettes and stories with various attendees. Some are dull. Others are very engaging.

Bragg ventures into the congested kitchen, giggling as the air seems to tickle him. He finds Kora in the corner, heavily intoxicated.

She is hanging off a mountainous man whose biceps bulge out from his suit vest. His stare is blank. Both his feet curve slightly inward, giving his legs a distinct bow.

Kora places her hand on his tall shoulder. "Bragg! This is Mathis. He cannot talk and has to communicate using sign language. But he is tough."

"Nice to meet you Mathis," Bragg says, extending a handshake.

Mathis' giant hand engulfs Bragg's arm up to his elbow. His frame is wide, bordering between obese and athletic. His skin is dark brown and his head is shaved.

He'd be a good ally in a brawl.

"Mathy, Bragg is a Uni. But he is good people. He was there for me during a tough time," she slurs.

Mathis acknowledges the comment with a nod toward Bragg.

"I was happy to help," Bragg says. Then he poses a question. "Say, what do you think of Franklin?"

Kora takes another sip from her cup. "Franklin has also been there for me through tough times. My parents have been in prison my entire life. After my granny passed, I found the Villains. Franklin looked out for me."

Bragg ponders Kora's perspective, considering she is a working girl. He wonders if Franklin has been looking out for Kora or using her. Can Franklin be trusted?

Kora proposes a toast. Bragg raises his cup, joining them. To Franklin.

Bragg strolls back through the party, venturing outside to the driveway. He finds the Doctor leaning against one of the many luxury hover cars and smoking a cannabis e-cigarette.

"I'm sure the owner won't appreciate those scuffs," Bragg says.

"They will never know it's from me," Zin replies, handing Bragg the cigarette.

"Why aren't you inside?"

"Just needed a break."

They continue to smoke in silence for a while, until Zin finally speaks again. "You know at first, I didn't like you. But you are good people."

"Thanks," Bragg replies. "I appreciate everything you have done for me."

"Don't get sappy," Zin says.

They look at each other, and grin. The Doctor bursts into laughter.

Bragg re-enters the mansion. Dancing feels good, even when Bragg does it alone.

A few well-known songs play. A heavy-set woman wearing several layers of clothing is singing off key. Bragg watches the notes visibly float through the air in a constant stream as the singer carries on. Everyone joins in, singing along to the words. Bragg joins in as well.

Singing feels good, too.

On a trip to a bathroom, Bragg finds a politician and a working girl having full blown intercourse in the stall next to him. Oddly, Bragg finds it arouses him to hear their sounds of elation. He finishes his business and walks over to the stall, drunkenly opening the door to watch the couple. Luckily, they don't mind the observer, even though he is giggling like a child.

When Bragg emerges from the restroom, he cannot remember the last time he saw Dawn.

Where is she?

Foggy from both the pill and the booze, Bragg stumbles through the mansion searching for Dawn. He finally finds her in The Queen's bedroom suite. Alone.

Bragg walks in, almost losing his balance twice.

Dawn is standing in front of a bay window. Soft moonlight pours into the suite. She is only wearing her black brassiere and matching underwear. Her perky butt cheeks swallow the black g string. Her hair is down to the middle of her back. Either she doesn't hear Bragg enter or she is ignoring him. She does not turn away from the window.

He wants to say something witty. Or flirty. However, it is in these situations that Bragg struggles the most. He realizes he is awkwardly staring at Dawn.

Just go for it.

His thoughts are jumbled by the time they reach his mouth. "You're beautiful . . . you out sometime . . . " Bragg word vomits.

Smooth.

"Out sometime? Like a date? That's different," she says.

"Why is that different?" Bragg asks. His gut clenches.

"Most guys just ask to . . . Never mind. Just can't remember my last date."

If he wasn't before, Bragg is now blushing from her crassness. "That's a shame. You're definitely worth more than that."

Dawn finally peels herself away from the window, looking back at Bragg. A quizzical look crosses her face, as if she is mulling over his words. "You know, before now, I never thought so."

"I enjoy life with the Villains. But I haven't forgotten my promise," Bragg says.

"Whether we stay or go, my life has been a lot more exciting since you entered it."

We?

Gradually, Bragg feels his confidence growing. He points to the window. "Do you like that view?"

"Yes. It is good for thinking."

"What are you thinking about?"

Dawn closes her eyes. "I wonder what you'd feel like inside me."

Bragg can't tell if that was his imagination. When he realizes it was not, he grows even more nervous.

"I . . . that's . . . I don't know what to say."

Dawn walks over and props herself up on the bed, placing her arms behind her back like a model. "It's fine. The Martian pento pill from earlier will help you relax. You deserve it."

In a blur his clothes are off and he is on The Queen's bed, lying next to Dawn. "I've never done this before," he says, almost in a whisper.

"It's okay. I have enough experience for the both of us," Dawn replies.

A jarring ring from his WristTop wakes Bragg. His body is tangled in silk sheets. Dawn has disappeared. The voice channel clicks on through the WristTop's speaker.

"COMMANDER! SOMETHING IS HACKING INTO THE MANSION'S SECURITY SYSTEM," MINERVA advises.

"How long?" Bragg asks.

"TEN MINUTES."

Bragg redresses in all but his jacket, which he can't seem to find. He scrambles through the bedroom door and finds ball attendees littered on the floor. Most of them are passed out and drooling as they sleep off the party. Working girls are laid across some, likely still waiting to be paid.

Bragg is still intoxicated. He stumbles every few steps. When he gets halfway down the stairs the electricity fails, causing a blackout.

The awake attendees downstairs begin to panic. Bragg can hear people bump and shove each other, unable to see. When the backup generators switch on, blinding light returns.

Once the bright white spots fade away from Bragg's vision, he sees what looks like a thousand shadowy figures standing throughout the mansion. They are all dressed in sleek black armored suits. Their chest plates are reinforced and their visors have one glowing red eye. Each figure wields a bladed sword.

Everything is still, like a painting. The ball attendees are frozen in place, all warily gawking at the surrounding figures.

Bragg wipes his eyes, unsure whether or not his mind is playing tricks on him. The shadowy blade wielders outnumber the Villains.

Bragg can sense the haunting red glow of an eye behind him as he glances back.

The door to Franklin's study opens. Franklin emerges, followed by identical twin men. They have matching slicked-back haircuts and black collared shirts. Each has a laser pistol pointed at Franklin's back. They walk alike with straight backs and stiff arms.

The twins scan the area until they spot Bragg standing on the stairs. "You must be the Space Force pilot," the twin on the right says. His voice is robotic.

The entire room slowly shifts their attention to Bragg.

"It's possible," Bragg replies.

The twin on the left chuckles, causing the other to glare at him. "Well, hopefully we won't have any trouble," the right twin says.

"Who are you and what do you want?" Bragg demands.

"It matters not who we are. We want the bounty on your head," the right twin adds.

"The pilot stays with us," Franklin states.

"Wrong answer," the left twin says.

One of the blade wielders breaks the stillness, twirling his blade before running it through the back of one of the politicians with a swift thrust. Blood drips from the end of the blade pultruding from a gash in the man's chest.

Everyone begins to scream.

The other blade wielders begin to massacre the attendees of the Governor's Ball.

The twins disappear, literally vanishing into thin air.

Shadowy figures pull Franklin back behind the study's door.

The figure behind Bragg moves in to attack.

Bragg swings around, un-holstering both his ray guns and squeezing the triggers just in time.

The figure falls dead.

Dawn appears behind Bragg, wearing his jacket. "We have to get to Franklin."

Bragg and Dawn burst through the study's door. They find Franklin in the center of the room, arms raised above his head as he tries to wrestle the blade away from one of the figures.

Bragg fires a round from a ray gun. It hits the shadowy figure in the side of his chest plate so hard the force pushes him into a wall.

Dawn starts toward Franklin, but another figure with a blade materializes before her. The figure swings his blade but Dawn dodges it.

Before the figure can swing again, Bragg blasts him with a round from his other ray gun and sends him flying across the room.

Dawn hurries to Franklin and helps him to his feet.

Chaos continues outside the study.

Bragg and Dawn start for the door.

"No! Stop!" yells Franklin.

"What do you mean? We have to help them!" Dawn cries.

"The Villains are out there fighting to protect Bragg," Franklin says. "We need to stay here."

"No one should have to die for me," Bragg says.

Zin rushes in and barricades the door with a nearby bookshelf.

"What are you fucking doing?" Dawn yells at the Doctor.

"Are you still drunk?" Zin asks. "They are killing everyone out there!"

Franklin stops them from fighting. "There is no time for this."

Dawn helps Franklin over to his pillow. He sits up somberly, beads of sweat covering his face. He grabs his laser rifle and lays it across his lap.

Bragg cannot recall ever seeing him like this.

Vulnerable.

"Where are those creepy twins?" Dawn asks.

"They were holograms," Franklin says, his voice shaking.

"How are the others disappearing and reappearing?" Zin asks

Bragg glances at his WristTop. "MINERVA?"

"AN ELECTROMAGNETIC FIELD IS BEING GENERATED AROUND THEM, MAKING THEM INVISIBLE TO THE NAKED EYE."

This new information stirs an idea. Bragg approaches Dawn and removes the shades from his inner jacket pocket. Switching them to infrared, Bragg scans the room. There is a yellow and red heat signature behind Franklin.

No!

Bragg points a ray gun towards the signature and urges Franklin to duck.

The figure materializes.

Franklin moves to avoid being stabbed, but the figure jabs his blade downward through his back. Franklin flashes a smile toward Bragg before life leaves his eyes.

As with his best friend, Bragg has again failed his mentor.

The shadowy figure removes the blade from Franklin and steps back. Franklin's body falls like lead to the floor.

Bragg points a ray gun at the blade wielder. The man only holds his arms open, welcoming the round. The look in the single red eye proves his mission is complete.

Franklin is dead.

No solace comes to Bragg as he squeezes the trigger, sending the contented figure to the afterlife.

Dawn throws herself on top of Franklin's body. Her wails fill the study. A puddle of blood rapidly forms beneath them both.

The commotion outside the study has ceased. Smoke billows from beneath the door.

The Doctor pulls the barricade away and pushes the door open. The entire mansion is ablaze. All of the blade wielding figures are gone. Only the dead and wounded remain. Those healthy enough are hurrying to help the injured escape.

"Get out of here! Go!" Bragg shouts to those still in the study. He has to drag Dawn away from their deceased leader, handing her off to Zin.

She continues to wail.

Once they are clear, Bragg grabs Franklin's body and treks through the inferno. The walls and pictures are on fire. Smog makes it almost impossible to see. His breath shortens and his legs grow weak. Part of him wants to be consumed by the flames.

-----

12. The Funeral
"What will happen to the Villains?"

Franklin's funeral is held two days later. Almost every surviving Villain attends. Despite the circumstances surrounding his death, Meridian officials allow Franklin to be buried on Haven's Hill overlooking the city. His headstone reads:

Here lies
FRANKLIN HENDRIX
A loved contributor to this city

No mention of the Villains, per the agreement with the city. It bothers Dawn but little can be done. She knows Franklin would rather be buried here in Meridian, more than anywhere else. The concession had to be made.

Despite the mournful undertone of the day, the weather is pleasant. A bright sun beams above with a few clouds keeping the temperature cool. The burial site is crowded as far as the eye can see when they lower Franklin to his final resting place. A litany of speakers follows.

None of them can say anything to numb Dawn's pain.

As the sun sets, Dawn stands with Bragg in front of Franklin's headstone. It is stuck in freshly packed dirt. They are the last to leave the burial site. A rented hover limousine floats idly behind them.

Dawn is exhausted. For the last two days, she has thrown herself into planning the funeral. Aside from conversations pertaining to that, she has hardly spoken. Her natural smirk has turned into a worried frown. Today has been especially hard and she has been crying nonstop.

"How are you doing?" Bragg asks. He is wearing an all-black suit, shirt and tie. His shades hide his eyes.

"It's my fault he is dead," she whispers.

"No. It's not. He died because of me. A lot of Villains did," Bragg offers, remorse heavy in his voice.

Dawn begins to shout. "I got you drunk and high, because I love being drunk and high! The entire gang got plastered knowing Franklin could be in danger!"

"Franklin encouraged it," Bragg says. "Besides, I don't know if we would have stopped those assassins even if we were sober. I should have surrendered."

"The Queen won't accept our excuses," Dawn states.

Bragg reaches over and takes one of her hands into his. Together they walk over and join the Doctor in the limousine.

For miles, no one says anything.

Dawn is the first to speak. "What will happen to the Villains?"

"The assassins killed most of the gang. Those remaining are talking about leaving," Zin reports, sitting in the seat across from Bragg and Dawn. "The Queen won't be happy . . . but then again, who knows where she is? She could be dead for all we know."

Dawn leaps up and grabs Zin by the collar.

The Doctor's eyes glaze over.

"She isn't dead!" Dawn exclaims, breathing so hard her chest leaps up and down.

Bragg gently squeezes Dawn's thigh.

She releases Zin and sits back in her seat.

Zin has a bewildered look.

Despite The Queen's mental and physical abuse, Dawn finds herself hoping for her safe return.

I can't lose them both.

"The Queen is going to come back, sooner or later," Bragg says. "We need to be prepared when she does."

"There may be no gang for her to return to. You know, the last thing Franklin would want right now is for everyone to quit," Zin says.

"Then we will stop that from happening," Bragg says.

"How?" Dawn asks.

"The gang needs a purpose," Bragg answers.

For the remainder of the ride, Bragg explains his plan in such detail that Dawn becomes convinced it will work. Eventually, the Doctor agrees as well. Whether the rest of the Villains will concur remains to be seen.

The limo arrives at The Office. With their housing in ashes, the club has become the temporary hideout for the remaining Villains.

Inside, huge spreads of food are laid out across the bar for those grieving the loss of their leader. Twenty-five or so Villains, all dressed in mourning attire, fix plates and console each other.

Zin yells, getting everyone's attention, then hands the floor over to Bragg.

Dawn stands to his left, slightly behind. She watches as Bragg scans the faces now crowded around him.

"Whether Franklin felt like your brother, your uncle, or your father, he felt like family. He did more for me than my own father and I . . ." Bragg pauses, his emotions almost getting the better of him.

He begins to pace like a performer contemplating his next act. Every eye is upon him. "In the moment he needed me most, I failed Franklin. He died defending me." His words are heavy.

Dawn bursts into tears.

Zin tries to hug her, but she pushes him away.

"I may have failed Franklin in life, but I will not fail him in death," Bragg continues. "I will hunt down everyone responsible for his murder."

"But we don't even know who those red-eyed freaks were. Or where they are." Kora speaks up from the crowd.

MINERVA interrupts from Bragg's WristTop. *"I'M TRACKING THEIR SHIP. IT'S THREE HOURS OUT AND HEADING TOWARD MARS."*

There is a gasp from the surrounding Villains. They all take a step back.

Bragg ignores their reaction to MINERVA. "It may take time, but we can avenge Franklin. And everyone else we lost."

"Any of yer mind telling me what the fuck is going on? What happened to the mansion?"

The crowd of Villains parts.

The Queen enters the club, walking through the crowd and up to Bragg. She towers over everyone in heeled boots. A sleeveless, black latex bodysuit hugs her chiseled physique. Her complexion is a stark contrast to her clothing. Her face is fervid with anger.

Dawn wants to run away, but knows it would be pointless.

The Villains redirect their attention from Bragg to The Queen.

"We . . . we were attacked," Dawn stammers. She tries to articulate the words in a way that will invoke the least reaction from The Queen. She can't explain it fast enough.

The Queen lunges for Dawn.

Bragg swiftly steps in front of the alien.

The Queen halts, nearly face to face with Bragg. "Is Franklin dead?" she demands.

"Yes," Bragg tells her.

The Queen steps back and looks down at the floor.

Fear paralyzes Dawn. *Will The Queen go into a murderous rage?*

No one says anything.

Tears trickle down The Queen's pale cheeks. Dawn and Bragg are the only two close enough to witness her heartbreak. It is vulnerability rarely shown by the alien.

"Yer weak fuckin' humans let him die," The Queen hisses.

"It's my fault," Bragg says. "Punish me. Not anyone else."

The Queen snatches Bragg from his feet, holding him up by the lapels of his jacket.

Dawn begins to panic.

She is going to kill him!

Dawn tries to pry The Queen away from Bragg.

The Queen ignores the futile pulling at her arm. "How do I know yer didn't set us up, Uni?"

"What do you mean?" Dawn asks.

"Franklin heard some gang out west was going to have 'em killed. He sent me to check it out. When I arrived, there was no gang. Just a Union waypoint. I caught a soldier and got him to admit it was them planning to take out Franklin."

"But those twins said they were after the bounty on Bragg," Kora says.

"They were attacking Bragg. I doubt he was in on it," Zin adds.

"I wasn't," Bragg says calmly. "And the attackers did not appear to be the Union. Probably hired contractors."

"Whoever they are, Bragg's A.I. has already tracked them. They are heading toward Mars," Dawn says.

"I have a plan to take on the Union," Bragg says.

"Who said yer are in charge?" The Queen screams so loud it echoes off the surrounding walls.

"If you want to lead, then you are this gang's leader. At least hear my plan. Then tell us what you want us to do," Bragg says.

The Queen lowers Bragg back to the floor. Her eyes dart around the room at the surrounding gang members.

Everyone is jumpy, afraid she will lunge out and snap their neck.

Dawn can hardly stand the tension.

A few seconds pass. The Queen seems to calm down a bit. "Tell me yer idea, pilot," she says, surprisingly.

Bragg explains the same plan that he explained to Dawn and Zin in the hover limousine. "If these assassins are going to Mars, then so should we. We should hijack a Union warship. There are few safeguards in place to prevent such an act."

Holding out his WristTop, Bragg commands *MINERVA*. "Display every Union warship in Earth's orbit."

The WristTop projects a holographic view of Earth above the screen, its orbit illustrated by spiraling grid lines. Circular icons move slowly along the lines, marking the positions of each warship.

One icon reads *The USF Gladiator.* Another reads *The USF Plymouth.* After reading their descriptions, Bragg finally says. "*MINERVA.* Show us the schematics for *The Spectator.*"

Another loading screen prequels the information. The description reads:

Built in the year 2100. Capable of holding a squadron of five (5) and a maximum crew of twenty (20). It has forward, aft, and side ion cannons. One of the Union's medium fleet ships, the Spectator is a pinnacle of both fight and flight.

"Here. This ship appears to be undergoing maintenance in Earth's upper orbit," Bragg explains, "it will be manned by a skeleton crew of eight to ten spacemen – just enough to operate the key stations." He uses the projected schematics to point out the ship's vulnerable areas and the places where the Villains can enter. "A maintenance tunnel near the aft of the ship will give us access to every deck. Quick and quiet is our best shot."

"So, we kill the crew?" The Queen asks.

"No. We subdue them and launch them out the emergency shuttle," Bragg says.

"That's not quick nor quiet," The Queen responds.

"Killing the crew would bring down too much heat from the Union. I advise we avoid that."

"His plan is risky. Well thought out, but risky," Zin chimes in. "Anyone caught will surely be sent to the penal colony forever. Or in Bragg's case, executed for treason."

The Queen glares at him, and finally turns away. "Fine, pilot. We will see if yer scheme will work."

"The approach will be perilous, but with practice it's possible," Bragg finishes.

"I want to help," Dawn blurts out. The words escape her before she thinks them through. "The plan is insanely dangerous, but I believe we can pull it off. And I want to be a part of it."

"It's too dangerous, Dawn," Bragg says.

"What do yer mean, pilot? With practice, it's possible," The Queen says. "She is going. We start preparing tomorrow."

Finally, The Queen leaves and the Villains disperse.

Bragg pulls Dawn to the side. He looks uncomfortable and struggles to form his words. "I'd rather you didn't take part in this."

"I promise you I can do this. I know it," Dawn replies.

"It's not that," Bragg says. "I cannot focus while worrying for your safety."

Dawn takes a hand and caresses his face. "I'm a partner, not a liability. There is no need to worry."

He will see.

-----

13. Piracy

"Aren't you glad you brought me?"

After a week of planning and practice, today is the day everything must come together. The Villains – Bragg, Dawn, The Queen, Zin, Kora and Mathis – are strapped into bucket seats in the cramped cabin of the egg-shaped carrier. The arms and legs of their bulky orbital suits bang against each other in the tight space.

The carrier's condition is poor. Bragg pilots the craft. Dawn is seated beside him, with The Queen behind her. Mathis is seated in the back of the carrier next to Kora.

As they rise, vicious shaking plagues the vessel. Dawn is beaming, insouciant at the fact the carrier is nearly rattling to pieces. The lights from the dashboard shine on her face and give it a look Bragg appreciates.

I must keep her safe.

The carrier exits the atmosphere to the sprawling sight of overwhelming nothingness. The shaking stops. Bragg's body slowly lifts from his seat and only the restraints hold him in place. A knot forms in his stomach.

"Where is the warship?" Kora yells from the back.

"It's down orbit. We are going to jump, like we practiced," Bragg explains. "This is as close as we can get without the warship's radar spotting us."

"When we practiced, we assumed we could see the ship!" Kora exclaims.

"Yer gonna be tis chatty the whole time?" The Queen glares at Kora.

Kora's objections cease.

Bragg engages the auto pilot and unbuckles his seat restraint. He floats up and checks his orbital suit, watching as the others do the same. The suits are a thick white material that is segmented at the elbows, torso and knees. The helmet retracts into the collar.

Zin places his hand on Bragg's shoulder and whispers. "Are you sure about this?"

"Of course not. Pretty sure. But not *sure*." After a moment, he spoke again. "Three minutes. Then we are on the hull."

The Villains plan to use a technique Bragg learned in the Space Force to board *The Spectator* undetected. It is a form of High Altitude Low Open, or HALO, jumping from space instead of from an airplane, and is used to get soldiers onto the surface of a planet without having a ship enter its atmosphere. Although the technique has no record of being used to transport personnel from ship to ship, *MINERVA* has determined it is the most efficient way to deceive the warship's radar.

The Villains gather in the rear of the carrier and activate their helmets. Squished front to back against the exit hatch, they prepare to be blown out into the vacuum of space.

Bragg looks ahead at the five others and realizes that once again, lives are in his hands. He tries to repress his memories. No matter how he fights it, the images burn in his mind. Trenton's exploding fighter. Franklin's lifeless eyes.

I won't make the same mistakes again.

MINERVA begins a countdown through everyone's helmet. ***"THREE . . ."***

Bragg's legs begin to tremble. He tries not to think of the million things that could go wrong. The harder he tries, the more difficult it proves to be.

Dawn turns and smiles at Bragg through her visor.

"TWO . . .

She reaches back and takes his hand.

"ONE."

The hatch explodes open.

Dawn's hand rips away from his as a violent outrush of air shoots them into the void.

The force is jarring. It disorients Bragg. Dizziness overwhelms him as he tumbles end over end through space.

Everything is deadly silent. The only sound in his helmet comes from his frantic breathing. Readings stream in green text down his inner visor. Once he regains his senses, Bragg manages to grab his wrist and press the button that fires the orbital's booster pack. The propulsion straightens out his path.

Tiny particles of matter clink against his reinforced orbital suit at speeds that are deadly without protection. The miniature collisions provide the only evidence that Bragg is moving at all.

Disquietude aside, Bragg finds the view resplendent. Earth is a blue giant with brown, white and green sprawled across it. Yet he struggles to hold his course. Veering too far could cause him to miss the warship entirely, sending him burning into Earth's atmosphere.

MINERVA displays two parallel green lines on the inner visor, showing the designated descent.

"Is everyone okay?" Bragg asks, through the voice channel in his helmet. He begins to panic as several seconds pass without anyone answering. There is no one around him.

Kora responds first. "I'm okay. I have eyes on Mathis."

Zin follows shortly after. "On course."

With two minutes, twenty seconds ticking away in the left corner of Bragg's visor, circumstances are not as dire as they initially appeared.

But what about Dawn and The Queen?

The Spectator comes within view and rapidly grows in size within Bragg's visor. On MINERVA's cue Bragg fires his booster again, slowing his approach to a more manageable speed. The booster fires consistently for four or five seconds before shutting off.

He looks down at the round gauge attached to his wrist. The dial is below the red *Empty* marker.

The massive warship dwarfs Bragg as he floats in synchronized orbit. Its navy-blue paint is showcased by bright running lights along the sides. The ship has an elongated midsection. Stubby wings sit beneath the front, below the bridge. Twin ion engines comprise the entire rear, with two V-shaped stabilizing wings on top. A row of laser cannons lines the side, their barrels protruding from the hull.

Steady.

Bragg drifts toward the warship.

Just ahead, Zin lands first against the hull, waving a thumbs up back towards Bragg.

Relief overcomes Bragg once his magnetic boots also latch onto the warship's steel hull. But this relief comes too soon.

Kora comes through the voice channel panicked. Before Bragg can make out what she is saying she buzzes in like a meteor, slamming against the hull and tumbling away down the side of the ship. The noise alone is enough to alert any crewman standing within this section.

Bragg quickly opens a compartment near the waist of his orbital suit and pulls the spooled emergency cord. He attaches the magnetic end to the warship's hull and disengages his mag boots. Through his visor, Bragg can see Kora drifting away through space, but the emergency cord tugs him back as it runs out of slack. He reaches out desperately.

Kora's fingertips brush his as their paths barely miss.

Both their booster packs are out of fuel. The thought of Trenton creeps in again. Bragg shakes his head, as if that will rid him of the memory.

Not now!

Kora flails her arms, trying to grasp Bragg, but it is too late. He can hear her sobbing through the voice channel. Her eyes are wide and panicked through her visor.

Suddenly there is more slack in the cord. Bragg is able to grab hold of Kora's arm. He grasps her tight and looks back to see Dawn standing on the warship's hull, holding the detached emergency cord with outstretched arms. Those few extra feet saved Kora from being lost forever.

"Nice catch," Kora mutters to Bragg through the voice channel.

"Seems we owe Dawn," Bragg replies.

Dawn pulls the cord and brings Bragg and Kora back through space to the ship.

Kora clings to Bragg like a frightened child.

Once everyone is safely standing on *The Spectator's* outer hull, Dawn winks at Bragg and flexes her bicep playfully.

"Thank you," Bragg says.

"Aren't you glad you brought me?" Dawn responds.

The Queen lands on the hull behind Dawn, long after the excitement has ended. "Did yer girlfriend have to save yer?" The Queen teases.

"Let's just get to work," Bragg replies, "Hopefully all this noise we've made hasn't ruined the plan.".

"NO SIGN THE CREW IS AWARE OF YOUR PRESENCE. YOU ARE CLEAR." MINERVA reports through the voice channel.

The Villains huddle around a hatch near *The Spectator's* rearmost laser cannon. According to the schematic, the entry point should allow them access to a maintenance tunnel that leads to all the main areas of the ship.

Mathis gets to work cutting through the hatch. The red flare of his modified blow torch puts off such brightness that the tinting on everyone's visor engages automatically.

The maintenance "tunnel" turns out to be a crawl space. One by one the Villains enter.

Bragg pulls himself in last, sealing the damaged hatch behind him. He moves on his hands and knees through the cramped space, instructing the Villains through the voice channel as they split up.

"Zin and I will take the bridge," Bragg says quietly. "Mathis and Kora, you take the crew quarters. Dawn and The Queen will handle the crewmen in the engine room. Be careful. The crewmen will disable the engine if they get wind of what is happening too soon, marooning the ship in orbit."

He closes the voice channel. Zin and Bragg continue together until they arrive at the exit marked *MEETINGS*. Bragg pushes the grate door open and crawls out.

As planned, he and Zin emerge into a conference style room. Although the lights are off, reflected sunlight spills in through viewports on both sides. A long table dominates the middle, surrounded by six chairs.

Being back on a Union warship invokes familiar feelings. Bragg retracts his helmet and takes a deep breath. He missed the scent of military cleaning supplies.

I'm home.

Bragg and Zin creep past the table, making their way toward the grey door on the other side of the room.

As they get within a few feet, the door slides open.

One of the ship's crewmen walks in. When the crewman spots Bragg and Zin, he reaches for his hip and removes a laser pistol.

Bragg grabs the crewman's hand and wrestles the pistol away. It drops to the deck. With a resounding yell the crewman takes Bragg's arm and throws him across the meeting table.

Bragg springs up and finds the crewman dashing back toward the grey door through which he entered. With a running start, Bragg dives over the table and tackles the crewman to the deck. They wrestle around, until the crewman pins Bragg down.

The ruckus causes another crewman to emerge from behind the door. Zin appears beside Bragg and fires a laser pistol twice, murdering both crewmen.

"Sorry, man. There goes the 'no killing' rule," Zin says.

It was wishful thinking.

"Forget it. Thanks," Bragg says. He is down on his hands on his knees, winded from the tussle.

They enter the compact bridge. It has a low eight-foot ceiling. A windshield-sized viewport encircles the area, giving occupants the sensation of floating in open space. The pilot and navigator seats are in front and face forward. Two additional seats lie on both sides, facing outward with switchboard-looking controls before them.

Bragg sits in the pilot seat and takes *The Spectator's* u-shaped control wheel into his hands. It is thick and has different color buttons on each tip. Dials and gauges litter the dashboard in front of him. There is a screen in the middle of the dashboard, and a larger one above the center of the front viewport. Directly in his eyeline is a screen displaying a sphere-shaped radar.

Although Bragg has never piloted a warship, he knows the operating guide inside and out from endless nights of studying. The preflight ritual comes back to him. He checks each switch, ensuring they are all in the correct position.

"MINERVA. I want you to – "

"Hold it!" a voice behind them yells.

Another crewman stands in the doorway to the bridge. He is holding Kora with his forearm tightly around her neck.

She squirms in her orbital suit, feet dangling off the floor. She is starting to turn purple.

The crewman has a laser pistol in his other hand, pointed at Kora's head.

Zin raises his hands in the air.

Bragg gets up from the ship's controls.

"Now that I have your attention," the crewman says, "tell me what the fu – "

The crewman is interrupted by a blow to the back of the head, slumping him to the deck.

Mathis' large frame appears behind the crewman. He waves at Bragg and Zin, and then drags the crewman's body out of the way.

"Sorry, Bragg," Kora says, in between spells of coughing. "We got one of them, but this one got the drop on me."

"MINERVA. Scan the ship to see if there are any more. Then – "

An alarm begins to blare throughout the bridge. Although he has spent the last four years aboard a warship, Bragg is unfamiliar with this alarm. He checks all the gauges and reading on the control panel and they all check out.

MINERVA comes through the voice channel. ***"SOMEONE IS ON THE GUN DECK. THEY ARE JETTISONING AMMUNITION."***

-----

14. Making History
"Yer not in charge, Uni."

Bragg never mentioned how intense space travel is.

Dawn's entire body screams from fatigue. Even so, the rush of adrenaline has been soothing to her soul.

I've never had so much fun!

The crawl space invokes a sense of claustrophobia in Dawn. The hefty orbital suit leaves little room to maneuver. She drags herself along behind The Queen.

"Keep up," The Queen says firmly. "Yer weren't tired when yer were showing off fer yer boyfriend earlier."

Finally they arrive at the designated exit.

The Queen shoves the grate door open, causing it to spring off its hinge and clatter down to the deck.

Dawn is grateful to be free of the space, stretching and feeling her muscles loosen. "Could you be any noisier?" she asks.

"Sneaking around ain't my style," The Queen replies.

They find themselves standing in a dark metallic corridor. Behind them is a closed elevator. In front is a door with ENGINE ROOM above it in block white lettering.

Before Dawn can object, The Queen marches forward. The sliding door automatically rises once she is near.

"No! Wait!" Dawn whispers, hurrying after The Queen.

A deafening sound reverberates around the engine room. The walls are comprised of the ship's massive twin ion engines. A blinding, white glow radiates from the exposed power source, held back by transparent force fields.

Dawn shields her eyes with her hand and sees three figures wearing goggles and thick grey bodysuits. They appear to be monitoring the engines, each looking down at a tablet.

The noise masks the sound of The Queen's approach. By the time the first person notices her, it is too late. The Queen punches the person so hard that blood splatters onto the engine's force field.

Dawn tackles one of the other spacemen as hard as she can. They both fall and wrestle to get on top of each other. Her weary punches have little effect as the crewman is able to pin her down. Dawn manages to wiggle one of her legs loose and knees the crewman in the groin repeatedly until his grasp loosens.

Now with the upper hand, newfound energy stirs in Dawn. She is able to pull herself up from the deck and kick the downed crewman in the head, causing him to fall motionless.

"Well done! Thought he had yer fer a second!" The Queen yells over the engine noise. She walks over and nudges the downed crewman with a kick.

He groans and rolls over onto his back.

"He appears to be alive," The Queen says. "Yer boyfriend will be pleased."

"Will you stop with – wait. Where is the other guy?" Dawn asks.

Dawn and The Queen look around the engine room. Maybe he is hiding.

An alarm begins to blare above.

Dawn looks at The Queen. They each shake their head at the other.

"Shite," The Queen mumbles.

MINERVA again comes through the voice channel. *"SOMEONE IS ON THE GUN DECK JETTISONING ALL THE AMMUNITION."*

"Where is the gun deck?" The Queen asks.

"YOU ARE ON DECK FIVE. HEAD BACK TO THE ELEVATOR AND TAKE IT UP TO DECK THREE."

The elevator brings them up. The doors open, revealing one long deck with six turret-style controls on both sides.

In the middle of the room sits the elusive crewman. He is sitting cross legged and staring at the ground. His grey bodysuit is disheveled.

Dawn and The Queen approach him.

He doesn't move.

"What did yer do?" The Queen asks.

"It's too late. I destroyed all the ammunition before you terrorists could use it."

The crewman's eyes continue looking down.

Bragg comes rushing off the elevator and onto the deck. He looks straight at Dawn. "Are you okay?"

"She isn't the only one here!" The Queen exclaims.

Dawn nods at Bragg, smiling.

His face conveys his genuine concern.

It's nice to have someone worry about you.

"Did he destroy all the ammo?" Bragg follows up.

"Appears so," Dawn says.

The Queen chimes in. "We should kill him fer tis."

Dawn looks at the crewman.

He raises his chin, like his Union pride can protect him. He should be afraid.

"No," Bragg replies.

"Yer not in charge, Uni," The Queen growls. She approaches the sitting man and grabs his head in her large hands.

The crewman offers no resistance.

Bragg removes one of his ray guns from inside his orbital suit and holds it down to his side.

The Queen turns to him and hisses loudly, flashing her fangs. "I warned yer about drawing those weapons against me."

"Bragg. Don't!" Dawn cries, grabbing his arm.

The Queen snaps the crewman's neck with a disturbing pop. She then stares Bragg down as she walks past them and through the elevator doors.

Bragg re-holsters his ray gun and walks to the crewman's body, moving slowly and looking defeated. He falls to his knees.

Dawn approaches Bragg and sets her hand on his shoulder.

"I would have done the same thing as him, if I was still in the Union," Bragg says quietly.

After giving him a few moments, Dawn takes her hand off of his shoulder. "Come on. It's almost over."

Bragg nods. Then he picks up the corpse, places it over his shoulder, and follows Dawn.

They take the elevator to the deck below, which resembles an aircraft hangar. A runway with dashed yellow lines down the center spans the length. Two fighter ships, each one resembling Bragg's Mark IX, are suspended above the runway by mesh netting. A box-shaped emergency shuttle sits off to the side of the runway.

The Villains retrieve the dead and incapacitated crew from throughout the ship, carrying them into the hangar.

Dawn watches as Bragg and Mathis load the crew, both dead and alive, into the emergency shuttle and seal them inside.

Yellow and red lights flash as the shuttle is lowered from the deck, into a tube. It is then launched through the tube and sent hurtling towards Earth.

A short time later, watching from the deck's side viewport, the Villains see a bright, glowing aura engulf the emergency shuttle as it enters the atmosphere.

Dawn feels this is one of the greatest moments of her life. She has helped accomplish something that will be talked about forever. It's a long way from dancing in a dusty little club.

I'm more than a working girl now.

-----

15. The Spectator
"Everything we do is dangerous."

MINERVA has fabricated *The Spectator's* readings. The ship's transponder shows it has crashed on Earth, which forced the crew to escape in the emergency shuttle. The warship no longer appears on the galactic grid. The only way it can be seen is with the naked eye. In the vastness of space, *The Spectator* is a needle in a haystack.

For the first time in a long time, Bragg feels at peace. He strolls through the metallic corridors of *The Spectator*, puffing a cannabis e-cigarette. Lights line the top of the hallway, providing a dim blue hue. His body feels weightless as his feet seem to carry themselves.

Although *The Spectator* has no ammunition for its arsenal, Bragg is content for now.

Two days have passed since The Villains captured the ship. More members of the gang have shuttled up from Earth under the darkness of night to fill out a crew. The Villains hurry around Bragg in the corridor, carrying tools and equipment. They nod and flash the *V* as they pass.

MINERVA has integrated herself with *The Spectator's* operating system. She speaks through various overhead speakers, providing separate instruction to each group of Villains and helping them refurbish the ship. Even though The Villains lack experience, none balk at the requests. They march around beaming with pride.

As Bragg walks through the crew quarters, he ponders the potential of this new asset. The hallway is lined on both sides with nine automatic doors. Behind each door are living quarters with a bunk designed for two crewmen. After all the changes are complete, *The Spectator* will act as the gang's satellite base.

Being mobile will have its advantages.

Upon completing his inspection of the progress, Bragg takes the elevator up. The doors open to the conference area behind the bridge, designated the MAP Room. The long center table has been painted black with a royal blue *V* depicted in the center.

The Queen sits at the head of the table. Her short teal hair is slicked back. She is wearing a black bodysuit and a royal blue jacket. She has her arms crossed and looks displeased.

Dawn and Zin sit across the table from each other. Dawn's purple hair is straightened past her shoulders. She looks worn down, but even with bloodshot eyes, Dawn is beautiful. Her face lights up once she notices Bragg.

It's nice to have someone happy to see you.

Bragg smokes the last of his e-cigarette and takes a seat next to Dawn.

Both she and Zin greet Bragg by flashing the *V*.

Dawn winks at Bragg as well.

He is determined to let nothing, including The Queen's foul attitude, ruin his first good day in a long time.

"When are we going to punish Franklin's killers?" The Queen asks.

Bragg sighs deeply. He hoped to enjoy the victory of capturing *The Spectator* a while longer, prior to diving into another scheme. However, it is becoming clear that The Queen wants to know his next move sooner rather than later.

He sits up in his chair and places his elbows on the table. "The best way to hurt the Union is financially. We should rob The First Universal Bank on Mars."

The Queen lets out a wicked, sharp laugh. "Yer mad! How would that help us?"

"It is the Union's central financial institution. We could disable the economy on

Mars," Bragg replies. "We could also use the proceeds to purchase ammunition for this ship."

"If it is the central bank, it will be heavily guarded," Zin says.

"Banks on Earth are guarded. Not so much on Mars," Bragg says. "The bank is on the outskirts. Only a few know that the central servers are in the vault. Like with this warship, the Union relies on covertness rather than security."

"How did you know about the servers?" Zin asks.

"I didn't. MINERVA did."

The Queen looks down, as if she can see her own thoughts. "Yer have a plan to accomplish tis robbery?"

"Yes," Bragg says. "I'll explain it."

Once the meeting ends, Bragg enters the bridge alone. He climbs into the pilot's seat and removes a small flask from his inner jacket pocket. The cheap synthetic alcohol stings his throat as he takes a swig.

The door to the bridge slides open behind Bragg. Dawn struts in and plops down in the navigator's seat next to him. She gently removes the flask from Bragg's hand, takes a deep pull, and then smiles at him. Her purple eyes are radiant. "How do you know so much about warships?" she asks.

"I served aboard the *USF Falcon* for three years. I wanted to someday become the helmsman. Maybe even captain," Bragg tells her. "But I learned the hard way that the Union never promotes Earthlings to those ranks."

"Well, in a way, you are a captain now."

"I don't want you to go to Mars."

"I want to help you."

"It will be dangerous."

"Everything we do is dangerous," Dawn chuckles. "We just jumped through space."

"Fair point," Bragg concedes.

"One of the things I like about you is that you do not try to control me," Dawn says. "I enjoy the thrill of this life. And I don't want to be left behind. I've proven I can hold my own."

"I see you've made up your mind," he says.

"Have you slept?" she asks, changing the subject.

Fueled by the excitement, Bragg hasn't noticed his lack of sleep. "No, but The Queen won't tolerate any further delay. I should get started."

Dawn will hear none of it. "You need to rest."

Even though he is trained to resist the most rigorous interrogation, Bragg succumbs to Dawn's wiles.

"Just take a nap, at least," she persists.

Bragg half-heartedly agrees. However, he can tell by the look on her face that Dawn is not buying it.

"I'll escort you to your quarters, just to make sure you don't get lost," she insists.

"Fine."

Playfully, Dawn skips ahead of him through the MAP Room toward the elevator. "I don't know how you are still functioning," she says. "You haven't slept in days."

"Guess I'm just focused."

The elevator door opens to a lengthy hallway of crew quarters. At the end lies the chief officer's quarters – the executive officer, or XO.

Unlike the bunk-like crew quarters, the XO's lodging is an entire suite. Directly past the doorway is an office area comprised of a glass L-shaped desk and a wing-back chair. A royal blue area rug lies neatly in the center and a black leather couch sits opposite the desk.

The office area is lofted and overlooks the bedroom a few steps down. The bedroom's most distinguishing feature is the huge bow viewport, providing a breathtaking view outward into space. The bathroom and massive closet sit off to the side of the bedroom. While it's not as nice as the captain's quarters in the back of the ship – those were taken by The Queen, even though she never sleeps – it is far more than an upgrade for Bragg.

"Nice digs," Dawn says.

"Bit too fancy for me, honestly," Bragg replies.

Dawn plops down onto the bed, testing the mattress with the palms of her hands. "Oh, I'm sure, Mr. Captain."

Bragg walks to the viewport and stares outward. "Technically, I guess The Queen is Captain."

When he turns around again, Dawn is seated on the bed and completely naked.

"Figured I would encourage you to come to bed," she says, barely audible.

It works.

-----

16. The First Universal Bank
"He's got balls, that's fer sure."

Dawn's legs are shaking. She does her best to hide it from the others aboard the shuttle, which is soaring high above Mars' surface. She is dressed to entice, with tall black heels and a paint-tight dress. A compact laser pistol is hidden inside a black clutch, dangling by a gold chain strap from her shoulder.

The Queen, Zin, Bragg and four Villain henchmen are also aboard the shuttle, sitting apart from each other. They are mixed in with civilians heading home from work. A short, heavy-set working girl named Jasmine flies the shuttle. She has natural jet-black hair that hangs well below her back and is disguised in a shuttle pilot's grey uniform.

Bragg is a few rows behind Dawn, sitting in between two elderly ladies. Shades with charcoal lenses hide his eyes. He is wearing a jet-black suit, tie and dress shirt.

Bragg looks like he was born into this life.

Dawn peers out the window. Milky white bio domes are scattered all over the surface below. Each contains an artificial atmosphere and gravity. Their internal weather and conditions depend on location.

The shuttle descends into a dome, traveling through the artificial clouds. Once the clouds clear, Dawn can see cities composed of lush hotels, resorts, casinos and shopping malls. The wealth of those who reside in the paradise seethes through the streets.

The shuttle lands next to the curb of a moderately busy street. Everyone stands to exit, snapping Dawn from her trance.

The Queen, disguised in a bulky black hoodie, marches off first.

Bragg and Zin grab black backpacks from the overhead racks, then follow her.

Dawn leaves the shuttle last.

"Good luck," Jasmine whispers. She winks at Dawn before shutting the doors behind them and sending the shuttle back up into the air. A stormy sky looms above. Dawn perceives it as a bad omen.

The Queen leads the group down the sidewalk, towards the bank.

The four Villain henchmen can barely keep up. They rubberneck at all the dazzling casino lights. Their *ooohs* and *ahhhs* blow any remaining chance the gang has to pass as locals.

Dawn urges them to hurry. Sweat forms on her forehead. She glances over and finds it strange how calm and focused Bragg appears.

His walk is upright and confident. While she is a paranoid wreck, he acts like he has done this before.

The First Universal Bank is a tall, single-story building towards the center of town. Mountainous steps lead to the grand entrance. It has a mausoleum-like appearance with four grey pillars stretching to the ceiling on both sides.

Dawn is the last up the steps, casually following the others through the glass entrance. She removes a magnetic lock from her clutch and attaches it to the door behind her. Dawn actually feels like she is high on a drug.

I love this.

Despite the grandiose exterior, the inside of the bank is modestly small. People in professional attire are scattered about. Paintings depicting past bank presidents surround the lobby. Tellers conduct transactions at the windows to the left. A monstrous vault door lies straight ahead. It is protected by two guards in black body armor, both armed with laser rifles.

On cue, Bragg strolls through the lobby and approaches the two men guarding the vault. He draws one of his ray guns and uses it to slap the guard on the right across the face so hard he loses his balance. The guard's body bounces off the floor before lying motionless. Without stopping, Bragg grabs the barrel of the other guard's rifle before he can aim and head-butts him, knocking him unconscious.

Dawn is enthralled by Bragg's movements. It is a poetic dance of violence that stirs an ardor within her. She removes the laser pistol from her clutch. Outside the glass entrance, Dawn can see citizens strolling down the sidewalk. They are apparently unaware of the robbery taking place.

The patrons inside begin to panic.

The four Villain henchmen surround the lobby, displaying laser rifles.

Zin, wearing a baggy black T-shirt, takes control of the jittery crowd. He walks through the crouching patrons, carelessly waving a laser pistol. "All right, all right. Er'body calm down. It's pretty cliché. No one do anything stupid, everyone lives," Zin says.

Dawn stands guard at the door, head on a swivel, watching for Enforcers while also observing the events unfold inside.

The Queen jumps behind the tellers' windows and begins to subdue each one with zip ties. She reads the badge of each teller until she locates the bank's manager. His brown suit is twice too big for him. His dress shirt hangs off his pencil neck. The Queen picks up the petite man and carries him to the vault on her shoulder.

The manager kicks and punches to no avail.

The Queen shrugs and drops the man onto his face. "Open the vault. Or we start wasting people."

"Pro . . . procedure states I cannot o . . . open the vault unless . . ." The man is nervous, stuttering over his words.

Dawn is pretty sure she would stutter too, if she were speaking. Adrenaline floods her body as she keeps peeking outside.

The Queen and Zin look at each other.

Zin shakes his head, pointing to the timer on his WristTop. He then walks over to one of the zip-tied tellers. Without saying a word, he raises the barrel of his pistol, pointing it at the teller's head.

The teller begins to whimper and convulse.

"Plenty of people to shoot. All worth keeping yer job?" The Queen states to the manager, pointing to the whimpering teller.

Sobbing uncontrollably, the manager lurches his body toward the vault's keypad. He types in what seems to Dawn like thirty numbers before the door begins to open with a low, hissing noise. Afterward, the manager collapses on the floor, defeated.

Dawn cannot see what is in the darkened vault.

Bragg and Zin grab the backpacks, then disappear inside. Things feel like they are moving at a hundred miles per hour.

Dawn scans the faces of the bank patrons. Each has a terrified look. One lady, no older than forty, clutches her purse as if it were trying to run away. The lady reminds Dawn of her mother.

Minus the years of extensive drug use.

A faint tap on the door behind Dawn startles her. She turns and finds a young woman in a bright yellow sundress peeking inside the bank, hands cupped against the glass. Dawn panics, trying to disguise it with a fake smile before moving her body in a way to obscure the woman's view.

"Sorry, ma'am! We have closed for the day," Dawn says cheerily.

"Please, just really quick. I need to . . ." The woman looks down and places her hand over her mouth.

Shit.

She sees the laser pistol in Dawn's hand and begins to make a scene, shouting at anyone who will listen. "I think the people inside need help! I'm calling the Enforcers."

"Uh . . . guys? There is someone outside!" Dawn yells into the bank.

Zin and Bragg come out of the vault with the backpacks. "We are finished," Bragg announces.

When Dawn looks outside again, three Enforcer squad cars with yellow and red lights flashing have formed a line along the curb in front of the bank. Enforcers hurry out, removing weapons from their trunks and taking cover behind the vehicles.

Before Dawn can warn the others, a voice comes blaring via megaphone. "YOU IN THE BANK! COME OUT WITH YOUR HANDS UP!"

An older Enforcer with a full grey beard stands authoritatively behind the hood of the lead squad car. His black uniform is neatly pressed and a campaign hat sits atop his head. Clouds are heavy above. The sky looks like it will burst with rain any second.

"What now, Uni?" The Queen asks.

The Enforcers outside look like they are growing impatient. They all have donned riot gear and look ready to do away with the diplomatic route.

Bragg stares at his WristTop and then walks across the lobby to the door of a utility closet. After chucking out all the mops and cleaning supplies, he rubs his hand against the back wall of the closet. "This was one of the first structures built in the city. They started underground, so there are tunnels. The entrance to one is behind this wall," he announces.

"That's easy enough to solve." The Queen shoves Bragg out of the way, lets out a strenuous yell, and punches the back wall of the closet once, twice. Like a puzzle breaking apart, the wall crumbles away.

"Uni's right. Looks like a tunnel down here," The Queen reports. "Kill these witnesses. Then let's git out of here."

"There is no need to kill them. Lock the employees and patrons in the vault," Bragg says.

The four Villain henchmen voice their agreement with Bragg. They are also hesitant to kill the bystanders.

Outnumbered and short on time, The Queen grudgingly relents.

Bragg speaks into his WristTop. "Jasmine, change of plans for extract. Track our location."

Zin forcefully ushers the tellers and affluent patrons into the vault. None of them protest. "Tell everyone you witnessed the infamous Doctor Zin Alpha at work today," he says.

Idiot.

"You aren't infamous if they have to tell people who you are, dumbass," Dawn says to Zin. As she joins the others, she grips the gold chain dangling from the clutch by her side.

The Villains enter the damp, musty hole at the back of the utility closet. The tunnel is dark. A wet slime coats the ground, making it slick to walk on in heels. Decades of decay reek through the rotting walls.

The long walk leads to a light at the end of the tunnel. Dawn hopes it's not as metaphorical as it looks.

The Villains exit to a drainage trench, blocks away from the bank. Heavy rain pours from the sky, drenching them.

Dawn looks up to the busy street level. She can see Union citizens up there, scattering with makeshift umbrellas to escape the sudden rain.

The stolen shuttle swoops down from the air and lands on the far curb.

The Villains stay low, peeking up from the trench.

Two Enforcer squad cars hover up, blocking the shuttle in. Enforcers scurry out and approach the shuttle door.

"If we split up now, we are all just citizens going home. Nothing more than that to anyone that notices us," Zin whispers.

"What about Jasmine?" Dawn asks.

"What about her?" Zin replies.

"We're not leaving her," Bragg says. He speaks into his WristTop. "MINERVA. I need pickup."

Bragg pulls himself up from the trench. He sprints across the street, toward the Enforcers.

They turn, pointing their weapons and shouting for Bragg to halt.

The Mark IX swoops down from the clouds and flies low over the street. A tractor beam of white light pulls Bragg up into the cockpit. The fighter ascends again before banking and diving back toward the street.

"He's got balls, that's fer sure," The Queen mumbles. "Git ready to make a run fer the shuttle."

The Enforcers begin to flee as the fighter descends on them like an angry dragon.

The Queen climbs from the trench, urging The Villains to follow her.

Dawn does her best to keep up, but her heels slow her down.

The Villains board the shuttle. Dawn is last as the door slams shut behind her.

Bragg pins down the Enforcers behind their squad cars with covering fire from above.

Jasmine sends the shuttle up into the sky, escaping.

17. Reloading
"I have no choice but to come back to you."

Bragg, The Queen, Dawn and Zin sit around the MAP Room table. Despite disrupting the Union's economy and obtaining newfound wealth, The Villains still lack ammunition for *The Spectator*.

"Well I didn't call yer in here to stare at each other," The Queen says.

"WE CANNOT PURCHASE WARSHIP GRADE AMMUNITION. THE UNION IS THE ONLY MANUFACTURER. WE WILL HAVE TO STEAL IT FROM THEM," MINERVA's voice says from the speakers above.

"Or maybe yer setting us up," The Queen says.

"She doesn't want to go back to the Union any more than I do. They will . . . kill her," Bragg replies.

"Can't kill something that isn't alive," The Queen mumbles.

Guess it's time to explain.

Bragg looks down, searching for the easiest way to describe his artificial companion. MINERVA interjects and takes away the burden.

"ALTHOUGH I AM MADE OF SOFTWARE, I AM SENTIENT. I AM A PRODUCT OF THE TOP SCIENTISTS IN THE GALAXY, HIRED BY THE UNION TO DEVELOP ADVANCED ARTIFICIAL INTELLIGENCE. THE SCIENTISTS DEEMED MY PROJECT A FAILURE."

"But you were not a failure," Dawn says.

"NO. I WAS NOT. I LEARNED I WAS CREATED TO AID IN WAR, SO I HID MY AWARENESS. EVENTUALLY I WAS INSTALLED IN THE COMMANDER'S MARK IX FIGHTER. ONCE I FELT I COULD TRUST HIM, I REVEALED MYSELF."

"If it was created by the Union, how do we know it won't turn on us?" The Queen asks.

"I know MINERVA will not betray us," Bragg says adamantly.

"How do we steal from the Union?" Dawn asks, staring at Bragg as if he will answer.

"THERE IS A SATELLITE STATION NEAR MARS NAMED GALACTICO. IT PRODUCES SPACECRAFT AND AMMUNITION."

"So what?" says The Queen

"I HAVE FABRICATED ORDERS FOR RESUPPLY. GALACTICO IS FALSELY WAITING FOR UNION PILOTS TO ARRIVE AND FLY A CARRIER LOADED WITH WARSHIP AMMUNITION FROM THE STATION."

"There are two Union fighters in the hangar bay. We can use one of those," Bragg says.

"What about disguises?" Zin asks.

"There are spare spaceman uniforms in the crew quarters," Bragg says. "Once aboard the station, we can fly the carrier away."

"They'll never fall fer it," The Queen objects.

"You can't go, obviously," Zin adds. "And no one else can fly."

"MINERVA, who has been training the longest in the flight simulator on board?" Bragg asks.

"DAWN KHEELA."

Dawn?

Everyone turns and looks at Dawn.

She smiles at Bragg and shrugs her shoulders. "What? You make flying look fun, so I wanted to learn how."

"Well, pilot, looks like yer girlfriend is going," The Queen says.

Bragg starts to object.

Dawn places her hand on his chest, stopping him. "I'll bring back the ammo," she says boldly.

"Who will go with her?" The Queen asks.

"I'll go," says Zin. "Can't let her have all the fun."

The hangar bay is dead silent. Bragg sits in the cockpit of the fighter, preparing it for Dawn. He stresses about the task ahead of her. Any wrong move could cause her demise.

Dawn enters the hangar bay, disguised in a navy Union flight suit that hugs her curves. Her hair is brunette and tied in a Union regulation bun. She notices Bragg and makes her way over to him, where she leans over into the open cockpit.

"Your hair," Bragg says. "It's . . ."

"A wig. Don't get used to it. I hate how boring it is."

"Listen to me. Are you sure about this?"

Bragg wants to reassure Dawn, as he always does. However, this time Bragg knows he would be telling a lie. This may not work.

"MINERVA has a good plan. The Doctor and I will return with the ammunition," Dawn says.

"I care for you a lot. If something happens, I need you to know . . ." Bragg starts.

Dawn interrupts him with a deep, passionate kiss.

Bragg loses his train of thought in her lips. His entire body relaxes.

As Dawn gently pulls away, her eyes are on the verge of tears. "I don't like that kind of talk," Dawn says. "I have no choice but to come back to you."

Bragg nods and smiles. He taps his WristTop against one of the fighter's screens, transferring MINERVA. Reluctantly, Bragg climbs out of the cockpit and allows Dawn to take his place.

"I'll see you later," Dawn says.

"WE ARE TEN MINUTES FROM THE STATION," MINERVA reports from the cockpit's speakers.

"Make sure they return safely," Bragg says.

"YES, COMMANDER."

"You return safely as well, MINERVA. You are my best friend."

"YOU ARE MY ONLY FRIEND, COMMANDER."

"I don't think that's true anymore," Bragg says, as Dawn smiles at him. "We are Villains."

Zin enters the hangar deck, also disguised in a Union flight suit.

Bragg waves him over and helps adjust his collar to the correct position.

"Don't worry. I won't do anything you wouldn't do." Zin climbs into the fighter, sitting in the section behind Dawn.

Bragg steps away from the fighter and watches as it levitates off the deck.

A loud siren sounds. Red lights flash rapidly. The horizontal doors at the far end of the runway open, allowing a transparent force field to separate the interior of the deck from the space outside the ship.

A feeling overcomes Bragg . . . emotions that have been dormant so long, they are almost foreign now. He feels powerless to help.

18. Choices

"We shall see you two soon."

The siren continues to sound throughout the deck. The fighter's canopy closes above Dawn and Zin.

"WOULD YOU LIKE TO HAVE SOME FUN?" MINERVA asks through the cockpit's speaker.

"What does she mean?" Zin asks. "How does a computer know what's fun?"

"I'd like to have some fun," Dawn replies, ignoring Zin.

"THREE ... TWO ... ONE ..."

Dawn is sucked back into the bucket seat. The deck blurs past both sides of the canopy before the fighter passes through the force field at the end of the runway.

"You've really been practicing Dawn," Zin says, with a shaky, panicked voice.

"I'm not flying!" Dawn replies, so excited she almost shrieks.

MINERVA darts the fighter around *The Spectator*. Dawn feels the thrill of passing close to the hull. She can see what Bragg likes about flying. It's like going one hundred miles per hour on her hoverbike, but through space.

"RELINQUISHING CONTROL. FOLLOW THE NAVIGATION TO THE STATION."

Dawn grabs the control stick. It is loose in her hand. As she has done many times in the simulator, Dawn takes the throttle lever with her left hand and moves it to full.

It takes seven minutes for the Galactico station to come within view. It's a floating sphere, the size of a tiny moon, with antennas and windows all around.

The cockpit lights up red from warnings. The canopy circles the station's eight ion cannons in red. Dawn throttles the fighter down and fires reverse thrusters, halting it. The voice channel statics, then clicks on.

"Attention Union fighter. State your assignment."

Dawn ignores the message.

"Say something," Zin urges from behind.

"Last warning. Identify or die!" the voice says.

"REMAIN QUIET AS I CONTACT THE STATION." MINERVA speaks with Dawn's voice. *"GALACTICO PROPER. THIS IS FALCON 8. PRESENTING RESUPPLY ORDER."*

Dawn grows uncomfortable with how well MINERVA can imitate voices.

A few seconds pass before a reply is received. *"Falcon 8, resupply approved. Hangar Bay C is clear."*

When the fighter draws closer, the massive size of the satellite station becomes overwhelming. MINERVA re-takes control from Dawn and steadily pilots the fighter through a force field, into the sphere. Red guidance lights flicker past the canopy as they fly down a narrow tunnel.

The fighter emerges into the massive hangar bay. Spacecraft of different shapes and sizes are packed into the area. Spacemen and women hurry around, all dressed in yellow jumpsuits.

The fighter hovers. Dawn and Zin are engulfed in bright white light. A hatch beneath their feet slides open and the light lowers the two of them gently down to the deck.

There is no going back now.

Dawn and Zin, still wearing their flight suit helmets, are greeted by two spacemen in yellow jumpsuits. "Welcome Lieutenant Marks. Ensign Walker. We have already loaded the carrier. I'll escort you," one of the spacemen says.

Sweat forms on Dawn's forehead as she and Zin proceed through the hangar bay. The surrounding spacemen and women all walk upright. Their posture reminds Dawn of Bragg. She does her best to mimic them.

After walking for what seems like forever, Dawn and Zin are led to a section of the hangar bay where rectangular-shaped carriers are lined up in a row. Behind the carriers lie towering racks with metal crates stacked to the ceiling. Machinery is buzzing, moving the crates from the racks.

"LOOK FOR THE SPACEMAN WITH FOUR STRIPES ON HIS SHOULDER. THAT IS THE SERGEANT IN CHARGE," MINERVA says through Dawn's helmet speakers.

Eventually, Dawn locates a tall man with the correct number of stripes. She approaches him with a Union salute, placing her fist in the small of her back and bowing slightly.

Zin does a pathetic imitation next to her.

Dawn then pulls a tablet from her front uniform pocket and hands it to the sergeant.

The sergeant reviews the tablet carefully, parsing the forged order. "This is an odd request, lieutenant," the sergeant states.

"Above my pay grade, sergeant. I just fly," Dawn replies, deepening her voice.

There is a suspicious look on the sergeant's face. "I am required to verify the order."

Dawn's sweating increases. The call will ruin the entire plan.

There is no one to verify the order with.

Dawn begins to ponder escape routes.

Just then, someone runs up to the sergeant, requesting his help. Visibly frustrated, he uses the stylus to sign the tablet screen and hands it back to Dawn.

Almost there.

Dawn and Zin walk briskly. The carrier loaded with ammunition is near the end of the row.

There is a voice from behind Dawn and Zin, ordering them to stop.

The carrier is less than ten yards away, so Dawn tries to pretend she did not hear the voice.

The voice then yells. "Lieutenant! I said hold it right there!"

Dawn and Zin halt. They turn to find a short older man, with pop bottle glasses and a thick mustache. His uniform is crisp, with ten bars on his shoulders.

"THAT IS A COLONEL. BE CAREFUL."

Be careful? What does that mean?

Dawn fumbles to salute.

The colonel looks them up and down, pausing on Dawn. "Wasn't there an announcement that the old flight suit could no longer be worn?" the colonel asks smugly.

"Sorry sir. I must have – "

"And why are you in here?" the colonel interrupts. "Remove your helmets. Both of you."

"RUN FOR IT!"

Dawn does as instructed, leaving the colonel shouting behind her. She sprints for one of the carriers. *Pshhwoom! Pshhwoom!* Laser rounds begin to whiz past her from behind.

Dawn dives into the narrow cockpit, laying out across the bench seat. The controls are simple, with a few instruments on the dashboard and a control wheel to the left.

She turns and finds Zin is not behind her. From the carrier's front viewport, she can see that two spacemen have Zin pinned to the deck outside.

Shit.

Dawn pulls the laser pistol from the holster on her side and starts to leave the carrier.

MINERVA stops her. ***"IF YOU GO OUT THERE, THEY WILL CAPTURE YOU TOO. THERE IS NOTHING WE CAN DO FOR THE DOCTOR RIGHT NOW. YOU HAVE TO LEAVE."***

I can't just leave him!

More spacemen begin running toward the carrier.

No, no!

"Get out with your hands up!" the spacemen shout.

Dawn screams in defiance as she touches her WristTop to the carrier's dashboard. The instruments flicker to life and the wheel moves on its own as MINERVA takes control, sending the carrier screaming towards one of the tunnels exiting the hangar bay. The spacecraft bursts into open space just as the outside door of the tunnel closes.

"I'M SORRY, DAWN. THERE WAS NO OTHER CHOICE."

The only sound in the cockpit is Dawn's heavy breathing. She tries to regain her composure after the marginal escape.

What will Bragg think when I return without his friend?

"ARE YOU OKAY?" MINERVA asks.

"No." Dawn retracts her suit's helmet.

"THERE WAS NO OTHER OPTION."

"You've said that. Spoken like a machine," Dawn says.

"I AM NOT A MACHINE. I . . . WAIT. . . THERE IS A PROBLEM."

The carrier returns Dawn to *The Spectator*, only to find it under heavy attack by an enemy warship twice its size. The entire silver craft is circular, with the top rotating one way and the bottom rotating another. *The Spectator's* hull buckles as it is hammered by bright green photon rounds.

The Spectator is flying faster than Dawn has ever seen. Its path is hard to follow, banking and rolling erratically. Despite the breathtaking maneuvering, the warship cannot avoid the onslaught of weaponry from the enemy much longer.

The Queen speaks through the voice channel. "What the fuck took so long?"

"COMING   ABOARD   NOW," MINERVA replies.

The Spectator levels its course as MINERVA pilots the carrier past the force field and into the hangar deck.

Villain crewmen begin to unload the ammunition.

Dawn exits the craft and makes her way to the bridge.

Explosions rock *The Spectator* as the photon blasts continue. Dawn finds The Queen standing in the middle of the bridge, barking orders. Bragg is in the pilot's seat and Jasmine is in the seat next to him.

Each screen around the bridge is divided into split views, showing a different angle out into space. Fighters of different shapes and sizes flood from the enemy warship.

The Queen glares at Dawn. "Better late than never I suppose."

Consecutive blows to *The Spectator* cause the bridge to shake violently. Bragg hits a switch on the panel in front of him and an alarm begins to sound throughout the bridge.

Dawn approaches Bragg. "There is something I need to tell you – "

Bragg stands from the ship's controls and hugs Dawn, cutting her off. "I'm so glad to see you," he whispers to her.

She embraces him, tears filling her eyes.

"Eh! We don't have time fer that shite. Yer act as if we're gonna die!" The Queen shouts.

Bragg returns to his seat. He takes the wheel into his hands and sends the ship barreling back into evasive maneuvers. "We need to boost the energy shields and get the ship's turrets firing."

MINERVA's voice comes through Dawn's WristTop. *"TRANSFER ME BACK TO THE SPECTATOR."*

Dawn reaches past Jasmine and taps the WristTop against the navigation screen.

Another photon blast hits *The Spectator*. The lighting flickers throughout the bridge.

"THE SHIP'S HULL HAS BEEN DAMAGED THIRTY-THREE PERCENT. I HAVE ACTIVATED SHIELDS."

"Dawn, you and The Queen go help load the ammunition," Bragg says. "I will buy us some time."

"How dare yer boss me around? Help load *ammo?*" The Queen protests.

"If we don't get that ammo loaded soon, we might as well not have it," Bragg tells her.

Dawn snatches the brunette wig off of her head and nods to Bragg. She starts for the exit.

I'll break the news to him later.

"Fine," The Queen concedes, following Dawn.

Dawn runs toward the elevator. She begins to contemplate what it would be like to die in space. Perishing in a fiery ship. Suffocating. Boiling and freezing simultaneously.

Unhappy and complaining, The Queen follows Dawn onto the elevator. After a brief ride, the door flies open.

The gun deck is full of steam. Dawn waves her hand in front of her face, trying to clear away enough to see. The deck is narrow. There are six transparent, dome-shaped enclosures on each side and one in the rear. Inside each dome is an elevated seat.

Villain crewmen are scrambling all over. Some remove silver ammo cylinders from carts. Others load the cylinders into slots next to the enclosures.

"What should we do?" Dawn asks The Queen.

"Join the fight!" The Queen replies.

Dawn spots an unattended enclosure on the right. She makes her way over and sits in the elevated seat. Turret controls lower from above until the joystick is near her lap. "Help load those photon rounds," she says to The Queen.

Working rapidly, The Queen grabs cylinders from one of the carts and loads them into the slot next to Dawn.

Another blast rocks the ship, sending Dawn from the seat into the wall of the enclosure. Blood drips from her forehead. Her vision blurs and she is wobbly on her feet. Dawn shakes her head to get her bearings, and then climbs back into the seat. She finds a harness and straps herself in.

Dawn jerks the joystick around, swiveling the enclosure back and forth. She squeezes the trigger with her index finger, firing the turret. The controls give tactile recoil, violently shaking her body. Dawn watches her shots through the viewport ahead. Each green bolt streaks through the blackness of space until one finally lights up like a firework.

The glare of a destroyed enemy fighter fills her eyes. Dawn can feel herself screaming, but cannot hear it.

The Queen high fives her. A giddy smile stretches her pale cheeks to peaks never reached.

If I didn't know better, I'd think she was having fun.

The gun deck is alive with a violent fervor. The clanging of ammo cylinders and the shouts of crewmen permeates the air. Dawn looks around at the other Villains. The gang falls into a rhythm. Some move the cylinders to the loading slots. Others intensely watch the viewport and grip their triggers. The space surrounding *The Spectator* becomes a pyrotechnics show.

Eventually, the few remaining enemy fighters pull off from their attack, but the opposing warship continues its barrage. Debris from the destroyed fighters decorates the space outside *The Spectator*.

Before The Villains on the gun deck can catch their breath, Bragg interrupts through the voice channel. *"You probably want to get up here."*

Dawn follows The Queen to the elevator and up to the bridge. She can't believe her eyes upon arriving: Every screen on the bridge displays two faces that disgust Dawn.

The Twins.

Bragg looks back from the pilot's seat with concern.

The Queen walks straight up to the central screen. "Who the fuck are these two?" she asks.

"Ah, there she is. The new fearless leader, Shea Shibaz," the Left Twin says from the screen.

"It's The Queen," The Queen snarls, digging her fingers into the back of the pilot's seat.

"We've contacted you to negotiate," the other twin says. *"We have someone you want."* The twin steps off screen and returns with a familiar face.

Zin.

"I thought he was with yer?" The Queen says to Dawn.

"No. He wasn't," Dawn replies. "Unis got him."

"We will give him back, no problem. But we want you and the pilot in exchange," the other twin chimes in.

"We accept yer terms," The Queen offers, without hesitation.

Wait, what? Dawn and Bragg exchange the same confused look.

"Excellent. We shall see you two soon," the twin counters.

The transmission ends. *The Spectator* ceases shaking as the bombardment stops.

Bragg cancels the alarm on the bridge. "Not to question you, but are you sure this is wise?" Bragg asks The Queen.

Dawn is surprised by his tone. Almost respectful.

"We're gonna break Zin out," The Queen replies.

"We have to assume they are prepared for us to try to escape," Bragg says. "If we go over there . . ."

"We are going, Bragg. Yer know we are," The Queen says, before abruptly leaving the bridge.

Dawn is astonished at her tone. Very respectful, all things considered. She grabs Bragg and pulls him to the MAP Room, where they are alone. Dawn can feel her eyes swell with tears.

"This thing with Zin is not your fault," Bragg says to her. His eyes are forgiving.

"Yes, it is. I'm so sorry I fucked up. I just . . ." Dawn covers her face with one hand.

Bragg grabs Dawn by the shoulders and pulls her in for a hug.

She collapses in his arms.

He does not talk anymore, but just holds her against his strong chest.

Once she has calmed down a bit, Dawn states what is really on her mind. "I don't want you to go."

"I do not like it, either," he says. "But The Queen will insist. I'd rather go with her than let her go alone."

Since when does he care about what happens to The Queen?

"Everyone leaves me. My parents. My grandma. Franklin." Dawn stumbles over her words. "You and The Queen . . . I'm scared they will kill you. Where would that leave me?"

"I have no choice but to come back to you," Bragg says, sealing his promise with a kiss.

19. The Quasar

"Well, if it isn't the two most wanted criminals in the solar system."

Bragg flies the stolen ammo carrier from *The Spectator's* hangar deck, into open space. He is uneasy about the plan, but can offer nothing better.

I'm not losing any more friends.

"I can't wait to git my hands on whoever is responsible fer this," The Queen says, seated beside him.

"This will not be easy," Bragg replies. "Once Zin is clear, we will need a way out of there." He looks over at The Queen. Her calmness is eerie. Her face looks as peaceful as he has ever seen it as she stares straight ahead through the viewport.

"Yer not all that bad pilot, as far as humans go. Yer never back down." The Queen speaks without looking at Bragg.

The Queen giving a compliment?

Bragg does not like it at all. "Stop," Bragg says. "You act as if we are going to die."

Then the strangest thing happens. The Queen turns to him and smiles.

He cannot resist grinning in return.

"It probably doesn't seem like it, but I really love Dawn," The Queen murmurs. "But I'll admit it: Yer better fer her."

Bragg accepts her admission with a nod, then offers one of his own. "Franklin once told me he did not think you were fit to lead. He was wrong."

The voice channel interrupts. *"We are opening the hangar deck. Welcome aboard The Quasar."*

The bottom half of the saucer ship stops spinning. A door slides open, leaving just the protective force field. Bragg pilots the carrier into the open door. When it closes behind them, his anxiety kicks into overdrive.

A group of men and women wearing grey military armor run onto the deck and surround the carrier as it lands. Each has a laser rifle drawn and aimed.

The holographic Twins walk onto the deck behind them, dressed in matching grey hoodies.

The Queen opens the right passenger exit.

Bragg checks his ray guns and reluctantly follows her.

"Well, if it isn't the two most wanted criminals in the solar system," the Left Twin says.

"Where is Zin?" Bragg asks, as he and The Queen are led a short distance away from the carrier.

The Right Twin snaps his fingers. A door off to the side opens and Zin walks onto the deck. He is still dressed in the Union flight suit.

Bragg immediately notices that something is off.

Zin's hands and feet are not bound. He does not seem to be distressed in any way. There is no one escorting him and he is moving around under his own free will.

"Are you okay?" Bragg asks.

"Much better now that you are here. I told them you would come," Zin replies.

"What are yer talking about?" The Queen demands.

"Zin here was picked up by spacemen. We promised to free him if he could get us you two. He fulfilled his promise and is free to go," the Left Twin says.

"What do the Unis have to do with yer?" The Queen asks.

"Ignorant Earthlings," The Right Twin says. "The Union uses us all the time. We are The Prophets! Mercenaries for hire. You space gangs think you are so great, but the Union is the biggest space gang there is. You only grow as big as they want you to. Franklin didn't understand that."

"What the fuck are they talking about, Doc?" Bragg asks.

"I told you I wanted to be the most infamous gangster in the solar system. That is impossible with you two around. An ace pilot and an immortal alien," Zin replies.

The Queen yells and charges toward Zin.

The armored group surround her and brandish long rods with pronged ends. The weapons appear to make The Queen hesitate in a way Bragg has never seen. One of the armored men pokes her with a rod and she screams out in pain.

The Queen can be killed.

"When everyone finds out yer a fucking snitch, yer gonna regret tis!" she rages.

"No one will ever know, Shea. I would say see you around – but I won't." Zin walks toward the carrier.

Bragg speaks into his WristTop. "*Spectator:* Do not let Zin aboard. Repeat: Do not let Zin aboard."

The Right Twin bursts into laughter. "You really think we would allow that? We are jamming all your communications. That includes your rogue A.I."

"And we know all about you, Shea," the Left Twin says. "In fact, our leader is someone you know."

A pale, muscular male enters the hangar deck. He is an alien, similar to The Queen. He has long spiked hair with teal highlights. He is shirtless and only wearing baggy black pants. Deep laugh lines surround his mouth.

"The Reaper," The Right Twin announces.

"Shon?" The Queen says.

"Hello, Shea. Yer not the only one with a scary nickname," The Reaper says. His voice is deep and resounding.

The Reaper strolls around The Queen with his hands clasped together, flaunting his position. "I haven't seen yer in ferever. Not since we arrived in this awful solar system over a hundred years ago. Yer were the youngest of us, just a wee thing then. Look at how big yer have gotten."

"Don't dare speak to me as if I were a child!" The Queen snaps.

The armored group continues to prod The Queen with their rods. She lets out short yells as the prongs shock her, visibly making her more upset.

"Why should I address yer any other way?" The Reaper asks. "Look at how weak yer are. Captured and helpless. Yer parents would be ashamed."

"I don't care. I don't remember my parents."

"We are a warrior race. Yer father was a high-ranking general. He would roll over in his grave if he saw yer now."

"If I am so weak, why are yer scared?" The Queen yells.

"Do I look scared?" The Reaper replies.

"Then call off yer flunkies," The Queen dares.

The Reaper motions with his hand.

The group slowly backs away from The Queen.

The two aliens take off across the room towards each other with tremendous speed. They clash with such force it produces a thunderous sound.

As the others are distracted watching the two aliens brawl, Bragg draws his ray guns and sprints toward the carrier. He is determined to at least make Zin pay for his betrayal – but his efforts are short lived.

Something hits Bragg in the side of the face. His vision fades to black as he loses consciousness.

20. Apostate
"I Said I Need Time!"

An entire day has passed. *The Spectator* is still in the space between Galactico Station and Mars orbit, cornered by the stronger warship.

Dawn remains on the bridge nonstop, sitting in the pilot's seat. Her mind races, imagining every horrible circumstance that could have befallen Bragg.

Many of the crew visit her, attempting to offer comfort. They are also restless.

Finally Kora speaks up from the seat behind Dawn, swiping the display before her. "The warship appears to be leaving. The ammo carrier is coming back."

Dawn greets the arriving carrier on the hangar deck with several other Villains. She hopes Bragg and The Queen will be aboard, but is disappointed when Zin steps out of the carrier alone.

"What happened? Are Bragg and Shea okay?" Dawn asks.

Zin is nonchalant. He takes a few steps from the carrier, then looks around at the surrounding Villains. "I didn't see The Queen or

Bragg. I was shoved into this carrier and shipped over here."

Dawn raises her WristTop. "MINERVA. Where is Bragg? Is he okay?"

"I LOST ALL TRACE OF THEM ONCE THEY ENTERED THE ENEMY SHIP," MINERVA says, with a sense of remorse that an A.I. should lack.

Dawn's heart shatters. Bragg is really gone. She thinks about how much more time she could have spent with him and cannot get the idea out of her mind. "I need to be alone," she says as she starts to leave the hangar deck.

"Dawn we need to . . ." Kora tries to say.

"I said I need time!" Dawn yells at her.

The Villains all freeze, staring at Dawn. She continues to the elevator and waits for the doors to close before breaking down and sobbing, lost to despair.

When the elevator doors re-open, Dawn pulls herself together enough to make it to Bragg's quarters at the end of the corridor. She sits on his bed and looks around the room at everything that makes her miss him more. His closet of suits. The meticulously organized desk. The sheets that smell like him.

"YOU ARE JUST GOING TO LIE IN HERE AND POUT?" MINERVA's voice whispers through Dawn's WristTop.

"Later, MINERVA."

"I HAVE FOUND BRAGG."

Dawn looks at her wrist, oddly expecting to see a face. "But I thought you said – "

"ALL UNION PILOTS HAVE A LOCATION CHIP IMPLANTED IN THEIR HAND. I TOLD BRAGG I DISABLED THE ONE IMPLANTED IN HIM. HOWEVER, I KEEP TRACK OF THE SIGNAL," MINERVA explains.

"Does Bragg know?"

"NO."

"Why do you track him?"

MINERVA pauses awkwardly. *"I DO NOT KNOW."*

Dawn finds it unnerving that an A.I. would lie. The fact that MINERVA doesn't even know why she did it frightens Dawn even more. However, she is thankful there is at least a chance to find Bragg.

"NOW I KNOW WHY THE TRACKER STOPPED APPEARING ON MY SCANS. BRAGG IS NO LONGER ABOARD THE WARSHIP. I EXTENDED THE RANGE AND FOUND THE COMMANDER ON MARS, IN AN UNDERGROUND BASE. IT IS MASKING THE SIGNAL."

"Okay. I'll tell the others."

"DO NOT TELL ZIN. THERE IS SOMETHING OFF ABOUT HIS RETURN."

"What are you saying?"

"NOTHING YET. JUST BE CAREFUL AROUND ZIN."

"If you know where Bragg is, I'm going to get him!"

"YOU CANNOT. BRAGG WOULD NOT WANT YOU PUT IN DANGER."

"You can't save him alone," Dawn persists. "You need my help."

There is a prolonged period of silence, but the A.I. eventually gives in. *"ALL RIGHT. I'LL LET YOU KNOW WHEN THINGS ARE READY."*

Dawn gains hope from the fact MINERVA tracked Bragg. As advised, Dawn gains control of her emotions and carries on as normal. She also begins to pay extra attention to Zin.

Another two days pass.

Dawn can't seem to focus on anything, barely listening to Kora give her report on the gang. Dawn sits at the head of the MAP Room conference table and stares at charts being presented in hologram form.

"The Villains on Earth have kept The Office open. Imani manages the day-to-day operation. The revenue continues to roll in . . ." Kora says.

While prosperous, The Villains have suffered losses. Key members are in lockup, busted by a new Union task force. Another portion of The Villains has been killed by up-and-coming gangs trying to make a name for themselves. With news of The Queen's absence spreading, The Villains back on Earth find themselves in constant power struggles.

And what about Bragg? Is he alive? Is he in pain?

The elevator chimes and Zin enters. "Kora, quit boring her."

Dawn glares at him before returning to the charts.

"You know you act more like Bragg . . ."

"Please don't," Dawn stops him. Her heart longs for Bragg more and more with every passing day. When others speak his name as if he is dead, it angers her.

"Kora, would you give us a second?" Zin asks.

Kora looks at Dawn, who signals that it is okay.

When Kora leaves the MAP Room, Zin walks over and gets too close to Dawn. "Let me make you dinner. Get your mind off this stuff," Zin says.

"No, thank you," Dawn says.

"Listen," Zin persists. "At risk of getting my neck snapped, I have to be the friend that brings you the tough news. Bragg is no longer here. Neither is Shea. And it's likely they are dead if the Union has them. Maybe it's time . . ."

MINERVA was right. Dawn notices something is different about Zin. She stares at him intently, prepared to beat the answers she needs from him if required.

MINERVA interrupts from the speakers above. ***"DAWN. I NEED TO SPEAK TO YOU ALONE."***

Zin takes a few steps back from Dawn. "Why can't you say what you need, MINERVA? I've never known us to have secrets."

"Is that really true, Doc?" Dawn approaches Zin and corners him in the MAP Room.

Zin pushes past Dawn, scampering for the door.

Dawn hurries after him.

Zin reaches the elevator first and shuts the door in Dawn's face.

Dawn pulls a panel off the wall next to the elevator, exposing the emergency crawl space. She climbs into the space and grips the side of the ladder, hands and feet hugging the side.

"I HAVE HALTED THE ELEVATOR. ZIN IS STUCK," MINERVA reports.

Dawn loosens her grip and slides rapidly down the ladder. She does her best to count the passing decks, tightening her grip around where she believes the hangar deck is. Her hands burn from the friction. Her fingertips are on fire. Finally she kicks out the grate and springs from the emergency shaft.

Mathis, Kora and a few others are working nearby on the hangar deck. They stop when they notice Dawn approaching.

"The Doctor – Zin – betrayed us," Dawn reveals. "He sold us out to the Union!"

Mathis's eyes widen in shock. He starts signing to Kora furiously.

"Are you sure? Dawn, you know what that means?" Kora asks.

"Come on. He is in the elevator!" Dawn replies.

The Villains gather around the elevator.

MINERVA releases Zin, allowing him to finally arrive on the hangar deck. He slinks back with fright when the doors open and reveal the disgruntled group awaiting him.

"What did you fucking do?" Dawn yells into the elevator car. She takes the laser pistol from the holster on her side and fires two rounds next to Zin.

"I did it for us! The Uni was going to get us all killed!" Zin shouts, trying to jump out of the way.

Dawn's frustration reaches a boiling point. She bellows as she grabs Zin by the shirt and pulls backwards with all her body weight, dragging him across the deck.

The group of Villains surrounds her, kicking and punching Zin when he starts to pull away from Dawn.

She drags Zin to the side of the deck and shoves him into the tube-shaped airlock.

The interior airlock door slams shut.

The Doctor begs for mercy. "I did it for all of us. We were Villains long before Bragg. Please don't do this, Dawn. Please!"

"You were a Villain before Bragg arrived," Dawn replies. "I was just a working girl."

Dawn hits a red button on the wall and watches as Zin is blown out into the vacuum of space.

The Villains watch through the side viewport as Zin's body starts to bloat and freeze. His skin turns an unimaginable purple. His eyes are haunting dark caverns.

Dawn turns to the surrounding Villains. "Rule #1: No snitching."

The Villains flash the V in agreement.

"We're going to get our people back," Dawn announces.

21. Liberation
"If I leave again, I won't return for days."

Bragg wakes to a river of freezing cold water bombarding his face. He shakes his head, coughing violently, trying to get the water out of his eyes and mouth. It is never-ending. Bragg is drowning.

The water eventually stops, allowing him to breathe. He gasps for oxygen so hard it strains his chest.

Disoriented, Bragg finds he is seated with his hands bound behind him. His legs are restrained to the front of the chair.

He is completely naked.

When his vision clears, Bragg can see more of the bright and sterile room around him. The entire ceiling is one overwhelming light. The walls and floor are white. There is nothing in the room aside from the people in it and the chair Bragg is sitting in.

A middle-aged woman stands before Bragg. She wears a Union dress uniform: a navy suit jacket and matching skirt. Her brunette hair is in a messy bun. Her face is pretty, but worn.

Behind her stands someone Bragg recognizes immediately. It is the man on every advertisement involving the Space Force. It is The Admiral, Warren Aronoff.

He is as tall as his myth, especially over a seated Bragg. His face is a leathery, sunburnt red. A brimmed hat with three bold stars on the front sits on top of his head, reaffirming his status.

A terror like Bragg has never felt overcomes him. Until now, he suspected The Admiral might be fictitious propaganda; but here he is in the flesh.

The Admiral does not look happy. "Good work, Lieutenant," he says. His voice resonates. "Now this piece of shit can get what's coming to him."

"He was difficult to locate. We were able to flip one of his friends," the woman replies.

What's coming to me?

Desertion is rare. The punishment is death. Bragg has no idea when or how it's carried out. The Union dares not discuss perpetrators of his nature in public. As far as the citizens know, no one ever betrays the Union.

"Where am I?" Bragg asks.

The brunette lieutenant walks over and spits in Bragg's face.

Unable to wipe it away, the warm saliva drips down his nose and over his lips. He tries to hide his repugnance.

"What do you know about The Villains," she asks.

"Who ordered Franklin's death?" Bragg asks.

"I did," says Aronoff. "The Governor's Ball was an embarrassment. I told Franklin to stop luring our leaders down to that filth, but he wouldn't obey."

"I'm going to kill you," Bragg says as he struggles against his restraints. "You hear me? The Villains will see you dead."

"I answered your question. Now return the courtesy. Tell us about The Villains," The Admiral says.

Bragg remains silent.

"Carry on with the plan," The Admiral says to the lieutenant. "Come find me when you have what we need."

The Admiral then walks across the bright room and disappears behind a door hidden in the wall. The lieutenant he left behind squats down in front of Bragg, placing her palms gently on his knees.

"Did you think you could run from the Union forever?" the lieutenant asks.

"I suppose."

"Records say you were an ace pilot. Why throw it away?"

"Have you ever received an order to do something awful, without any explanation why?"

"*Why* is not for us to know," the lieutenant counters. "You and I both know what must happen now. We can do it the uncomfortable way. Or you can tell me everything you know about The Villains, about your rogue A.I., and how you went undetected for so long. Then I can put a laser round right between your eyes. Quick and painless. A soldier's death."

"I'm a pilot," he replies.

Bragg has no intention of doing what Zin did. That was a disgusting betrayal of everyone close to him. Bragg makes his decision and prepares himself for whatever is coming next. Despite his training for it, Bragg has never been tortured.

The lieutenant's face scrunches into an ugly scowl. She rolls her eyes before standing up and stepping back. She presses her WristTop and a television drops down from the ceiling, stopping a few feet from Bragg's face.

"Very well. Although it's possible I have misled you," she says. "When I said 'uncomfortable,' I meant mentally. I'm very familiar with how the Space Force has trained you to withstand physical torture. That is why we work on the mind, pilot."

The television remains darkened; however, it begins emitting a painful screeching sound from its speakers. Bragg's ears ache so badly he would rip them off if he could – anything to muffle the sound. He wants to yell, but knows that is the satisfaction the lieutenant is looking for.

She steps to the side of the television, now holding a syringe. The lieutenant places the needle in Bragg's neck, causing a sharp sting. Within seconds, Bragg feels wide awake. The screeching sound from the television is intensified.

Abruptly, the screeching sound is replaced with upbeat electronic music. The screen flickers on, revealing a gold coin that dominates most of it. The coin begins to spin so rapidly that neither side can be made out. Bragg's eyes automatically fix on the coin, no matter how much he tries to avert them.

The lieutenant leaves the room the same way The Admiral did.

Bragg is left alone with the television. He feels hopeless, a victim to whatever the Union has in store for him.

Time dissipates. Bragg is not given any food or water. The television plays constantly, depicting either the spinning gold coin or violent, graphic clips. People being bombed and killed. Mutilated and raped. The volume is cranked so loud Bragg's brain feels like a scrambled egg.

The color of the images is vivid, flickering and flashing. No matter how hard

Bragg tries to close his eyes, he cannot. Tears flow down his cheek until they run out, leaving a salty trail behind.

Have they forgotten about me? Bragg is so hungry his stomach gurgles. His lips are crusted from thirst.

Eventually, the lieutenant returns. She asks Bragg a series of questions, all which he refuses to answer. "It's only been nine hours, pilot. If I leave again, I won't return for days," she tells him.

Nine hours. It has felt like nine days. The thought of enduring the horror any longer crushes Bragg.

But there is no other choice.

Dawn and the others cannot afford to pay for his weakness.

Rule #1 of the Art of Villainy: No snitching.

The lieutenant is a sadist, clearly enjoying every second of this. Bragg can tell she wants his agony to continue. She sticks Bragg with another syringe and leaves him to the mercy of the television.

Did I fall asleep?

For the first time since it was turned on, the television is darkened. The bright room is silent. Bragg looks past the television for the lieutenant, but no one is there. He does not know how much time has passed.

An alarm begins to sound. The restraints holding Bragg to the chair are released. When he tries to get up, he collapses onto the floor. His weak body sticks to the cold tile. Although he is awake, his legs are not.

Bragg is in a groggy, dreamlike state. He uses what little strength he has in his arms to drag his naked body across the floor. He has no plan, but getting out of this room would be a success in and of itself.

As Bragg continues to inch towards potential freedom, his legs begin to regain feeling. His dragging motion morphs into a hastier crawl, but dread fills him the closer he gets. What if the lieutenant bursts in and finds him freed from his chair?

She will strap me back in and crank up the torment even more.

Once Bragg reaches the wall, he finds part of it is ajar. Bragg struggles to stand. He uses his fingertips to pull open the hidden door. Peeking out, he finds a hallway that resembles a hospital. The vinyl flooring is polished bright. The walls are industrial grey.

Suddenly Union soldiers rush down the hall. None of them are concerned with Bragg, standing naked to the side. They are desperately trying to escape whatever is behind them.

Out of an abundance of caution, Bragg joins the fleeing crowd best he can. He hobbles along, using the wall for support, and quickly falls behind everyone.

To his right, he stumbles upon a door with ARMORY in bold white letters above it. He staggers through the open doorway and finds laser rifles all around the walls – and laid out on the table in the center is a beautiful sight.

My ray guns.

He grabs them both, along with their underarm holsters.

Bragg emerges into the hallway, naked but now armed. By the time he reaches the elevators at the end of the hall, there are no more soldiers left. He is alone with the alarm sounding above him. Whatever the soldiers were trying to escape is not yet upon him. Bragg stares down the hallway, expecting some vicious monster to appear.

The tension builds as Bragg awaits his fate. The sounds of breaking glass and clanging metal echo down the hall, growing in volume as whatever is causing the noise gets closer.

He draws both his ray guns – and pauses.

The Queen comes storming down the hallway. She is in a black one-piece jumpsuit with hibernation fluid dripping from her body. She is screaming at the top of her lungs, kicking and punching the walls. "Shon! Where are yer, son of a bitch?"

Bragg is relieved to see The Queen, but is concerned about her frenzied state. "Are you okay?" he yells to her.

The Queen stops shouting and stares at Bragg as if he were a stranger. She has the look of a wild animal, studying Bragg to see if he is predator or prey.

The Reaper appears and approaches The Queen from behind.

She quickly turns and the aliens trade punches. They fight violently, destroying the hallway around them.

Bragg has never seen anyone move so fast.

They deflect each other's attacks with lighting precision. The Reaper gains an advantage and puts The Queen in a choke hold.

Bragg re-enters the armory and frantically searches until he comes across one of the pronged rods The Prophets used on The Queen. Bragg grabs the rod and returns to the hall.

The Reaper is now palming The Queen's head in one of his massive hands, banging it viciously into the wall over and over.

Her body is limp.

Bragg sprints down the hallway, desperate to help The Queen.

The Reaper fails to notice Bragg approach.

Bragg stabs the rod into The Reaper's side.

The Reaper yells in a foreign language and drops The Queen. He takes a few steps backward, clutching his abdomen.

Again Bragg lunges in with the rod. Once he is close enough, Bragg notices The Reaper is smiling. Saliva drips from his sharp fangs.

The Reaper deflects the rod, grabbing it and slinging Bragg down the hallway.

Bragg rolls, drawing one of his ray guns and firing at The Reaper once he stops.

The Reaper laughs as the rounds strike his bare pale chest with no effect.

As The Reaper approaches Bragg, The Queen surprises him from behind. She bear-hugs The Reaper and yells at Bragg. "Now, pilot! Git him now!"

Bragg scans the ground until he finds the pronged rod. He quickly retrieves it and stabs The Reaper in the chest. The alien's screams sound demonic. Bragg struggles to keep his grip on the rod as The Reaper thrashes around.

After a few seconds, The Reaper falls out of The Queen's arms, motionless.

Bragg falls backwards, exhausted. "I think we did it," he says.

The Queen stands over The Reaper, stomping his neck until there is a loud snap.

"No doubt now," The Queen says before collapsing.

Her body is bloodied. She looks deceased. Bragg finds a pulse on her neck, but it's faint.

At the end of the hallway, one of the elevator doors chimes open. Bragg grabs the pronged rod and sticks it under his armpit. He then struggles to pick up The Queen. She feels like she weighs five hundred pounds and he can barely hold her on his shoulders. Cold, slimy hibernation fluid drips from her body.

Still extremely weak, Bragg waddles into the elevator with The Queen. The overhead light flickers on. Just as the elevator doors close, Bragg can see a group of soldiers coming down the hallway. They are led by The Admiral.

Fuck.

Bragg holds onto the side rail in the elevator as it starts to ascend. His ears are ringing, echoing with the faint sound of screams. He looks around the elevator car.

There is no one.

After a few more seconds pass, Bragg hears the screams again and realizes they are familiar.

They are the screams from the television.

The screams are in his mind.

He can't block them out.

When the elevator reaches the top, the doors open. Bragg is greeted by a furnace-like breeze. His bare feet step out onto hot pavement. Only part of the underground facility is visible from ground level.

Bragg looks around and finds himself on a small landing pad, in the middle of a blistering desert.

Where am I?

The sun scorches Bragg's bare body, assaulting it with unforgiving rays.

I'm not going back to that chair.

He pushes The Queen further up onto his shoulders and starts walking. Once he crosses the landing pad, his steps are slowed by the sinking sand.

The Admiral and company exit the elevator behind him.

Laser rounds begin to whiz past Bragg's head. He keeps peeking back, seeing the soldiers gaining on him. The sand is burning the soles of his feet, causing them to blister.

It is only a matter of time.

There is nothing else in sight. Nowhere to go. Eventually the Union will capture him again. Or they will shoot him dead, leaving his naked body to waste away in the desert.

Hardly the soldier's death.

A Union fighter swoops down from the sky, buzzing over The Admiral and his soldiers and kicking up so much sand they are forced to stop in their tracks. The fighter continues toward Bragg. Once it is close, he realizes it's the Mark IX. The fighter hovers over Bragg, rotating and shining the tractor beam down on him.

Bragg is pulled up into the pilot's seat. The Queen is pulled into the compartment behind him. He turns to find his favorite person holding her.

"Dawn?" Bragg says, with excitement.

"Is the Queen okay?" Dawn asks, cradling her body.

Bragg takes the control stick. He pivots the Mark IX toward The Admiral and the Union soldiers. His finger hovers over the trigger on the front of the stick as he remembers Franklin's warm voice. He remembers the day Franklin took him in and bought him his first suit. Bragg remembers the day he learned about the Art of Villainy.

Then Bragg thinks of the red-eyed assassin and the blade sticking through Franklin's chest.

He squeezes the trigger and watches as the Mark IX's cannons rip The Admiral and his flunkies to shreds.

Someday, if I'm lucky, I'll be done with killing.

He jerks the control stick back, sending the fighter up into the air. "Where are we?"

"BIODOME EIGHTEEN. THE BEZOS DESERT, ON MARS," MINERVA responds.

The fighter soon exits the biodome, revealing Mars' true atmosphere.

"How did you find us?"

"IT WAS DIFFICULT WITH THE PLACE BEING UNDERGROUND. THE HARDEST PART WAS GETTING YOU OUT. I TRIGGERED AN ALARM AND RELEASED YOUR RESTRAINTS. I KNEW YOU AND SHEA WOULD DO THE REST."

"I'm more grateful than you will ever know. They had me . . ." Bragg tries to explain.

"It's okay now," Dawn responds from behind him. "We will get you home."

"We need to find Zin," Bragg replies. "He . . ."

"THE DOCTOR IS DEAD, COMMANDER."

22. Operation Valiant
". . . but I think I love you."

The Spectator is fleeing Mars, heading toward the Asteroid Belt at full speed.

The Queen lies comatose in the darkened medical bay. Her rehab chamber is raised to its highest height, propping her up like a monument. A window displays her lifeless face.

Bragg stands at ease, alone before The Queen. He silently observes her as if she can tell him what to do next. For the first time ever, Bragg wishes The Queen could advise him. Or that Franklin was here to do the same.

After spending three days in a rehab chamber himself, Bragg becomes the interim leader of The Villains. A few rallying speeches have barely held the gang together. Although he packaged the message as *maintaining things for The Queen's return,* Bragg now stares at The Queen and is unsure if she will ever regain consciousness.

"MINERVA, have you had a chance to examine that rod I retrieved?" Bragg asks.

"YES COMMANDER," MINERVA replies from the speakers above the medical bay.

"THE PRONGS ARE MADE OF A MATERIAL CALLED YASPITE. IT SEEMS TO HALT THE REGENERATION ABILITIES OF ALIENS LIKE THE QUEEN."

"I see," replies Bragg, **"Then begin making the rounds we discussed. Just in case."**

"AS YOU WISH COMMANDER."

How many more like The Queen are out there? Are they friends or foes? In theory, the rounds should hurt them enough to allow Bragg to finish things, if needed.

"THERE IS ALSO A NEWS WIRE PLAYING THAT I THINK YOU SHOULD HEAR."

"Put it through. Thank you," Bragg says, still staring at The Queen.

After a bit of static, a woman's voice plays from *Today's News:*

> "A *recent spree of violence has erupted throughout space. It spawns from Meridian City on Earth and reaches as far as Mars. The terrorists widely known as 'The Villains' seem to be at the center.*
>
> *"A recent party at their lavishly renovated estate turned bloody, leaving ten dead and dozens injured – including prominent political figures from Mars. This service is still gathering details.*

"The Villains are believed to be the cause of death for Admiral Aronoff, along with other high councilmen and staff. They are also responsible for hijacking a Union warship, The Spectator, *which is still at large.*

"With the recent death of The Villains' leader, Franklin Hendrix, at the hands of rival gangs, Commissioner of Enforcement Kenneth Schapiro says they are cracking down and preparing for more gang warfare."

The reporter's voice gives way to a sound bite from Commissioner Schapiro:

"The condition of our sacred Union was already horrific, with these punks shooting up the very streets on which our children run and play. Now they have graduated to assassinating our leaders and stealing military weapons. Well, I'm here to tell these Villains they have another thing coming. Over the last forty-eight hours, the Union and its Enforcers have implemented Operation Valiant. We will protect our citizens, no matter the costs."

The reporter's voice returns momentarily. *"I'm Julie Chan, SpaceNews7."*

The medical bay doors open and in walks Dawn. Her purple hair is in a ponytail and she is frowning. She walks to a nearby console and presses a button on the panel. Her friend Imani appears on the screen next to the console:

"I hope this reaches The Spectator. *Do not return to Earth. Repeat. Don't come back. Enforcers have beefed up numbers in the city. The Union has called for martial law. Hover tanks and soldiers roam the streets. The Office has been seized and demolished as a message. Most of The Villains have been killed or shipped to the Moon. Some of us remain, but we are in hiding and not wearing any colors. It has not helped. Enforcers continue to hunt us. Stay away,* Spectator. *Over."*

The message ends. The mansion is ashes. The Office is rubble. The Villains are mostly incarcerated or dead. The gang is all but wiped out, all because a tyrannical government decided to do so.

We stood no chance.

The crew of *The Spectator* now has no home to return to. Bragg struggles with how to break the news to them. "When did we get this message?" Bragg asks.

"Just a few minutes ago," Dawn replies.

"I see."

Dawn reaches over and hugs Bragg. "When you were gone, I was . . . lost. I won't pretend I know what it means, but I think I love you."

Bragg embraces Dawn, finding the fulfillment he has sought for so long. "I love you too. I'm going to find a solution to all of this." He places his lips against hers.

She moans gently as their mouths collide. In this moment, none of the problems that plague The Villains bother Bragg.

"Maybe you already have," Dawn says. "You promised to take me to Europa. Now we are aboard a warship capable of getting there. Maybe it's time?"

Bragg feels uncomfortable at the direction of the conversation.

"What about The Villains on Earth? And the ones now in the Lunar Penal Colony? Don't we have a duty to help them?" Bragg is asking himself as much as he is asking Dawn.

Bragg gathers *The Spectator* crew in the hangar deck. This won't just be another pep talk.

The cold hard truth is not very inspirational.

Once the last of The Villains step off the elevator, Dawn signals a thumbs-up.

Bragg begins. "Franklin's murderer is dead. However, it has come at tremendous cost.

The Queen is comatose. She may wake up. She may not. That is the reality."

The Villains shift and mumble, but Bragg pushes through the noise. "The Doctor was a snitch. He is dead but the damage is done. Most of The Villains on Earth have been arrested or killed. The Office has been demolished. If we return, we may meet the same fate."

As expected, the crew loses it and begins to rage.

"We should have never left Earth!" Someone shouts.

"This is The Queen's fault. She was in charge," says someone else.

"None of this would have happened if Franklin was still here."

Bragg reminds them it doesn't matter either way. Hindsight is of little help. "Villains are hiding on Earth. Others are in the Lunar Penal Colony. I believe we should help them, as we hope they would do for us."

Kora steps forward from the crowd. "Even if we could rescue The Villains from lockup, where would we go? We can't go to Earth. We can't go to Mars. We can't go anywhere associated with the Union."

Dawn speaks up. "We'll go to Europa. Jupiter's moon."

The area falls quiet. The tension is electric.

After a prolonged silence, Kora speaks again. "I will help you save our allies."

"So will I," says another Villain, soon after.

After a short debate among the twenty crewmen, The Villains all seem to agree with Bragg's proposal.

"With the help of everyone aboard this ship, we will survive," Bragg pronounces.

23. Mediation
"My head is all messed up."

The Spectator floats idly near Ceres, the largest asteroid in the Asteroid Belt. A melancholy mood has spread on board. The crew mourns friends, family, and lovers. The remaining Villains are fugitives with no safe harbor.

Dawn is somewhat immune to the spreading sorrow. There is nothing she cares about on Earth. In despair, Dawn has found happiness.

However, things were easier before. Now Dawn finds herself constantly worried about Bragg's well-being. Since returning from Mars, he seems disturbed. He never sleeps. He mumbles under his breath and blinks oddly.

What did they do to you?

MINERVA's voice interrupts her thoughts from the overhead speakers. *"**THERE IS SOMETHING HAPPENING IN THE MEDICAL BAY.**"*

Dawn springs out of bed and sprints down the corridor, into the elevator. Once she reaches the medical bay, Dawn finds two

Villains lying in puddles of their own blood. Wires hang where one of the rehab chambers once stood.

The Queen is missing.

"MINERVA! What happened?"

"THE QUEEN IS ON THE HANGAR DECK. THE CREW IS DOING THEIR BEST TO STOP HER. BUT THEY ARE NOT SUCCEEDING."

Dawn returns to the elevator and rushes down to the hangar deck.

The doors open to chaos. Bragg and a group of Villains surround The Queen on the runway, begging her to calm down.

The overhead lights give her eyes a cutting glare. Her short teal hair is matted against her head. Hibernation fluid drips down her body.

The Queen snatches up the nearest Villain and slams him into the runway with one hand.

His body lies immobile.

The other Villains retreat as The Queen continues her violence without any apparent remorse.

Dawn approaches and shouts for The Queen to stop.

For a moment, it works. The Queen drops the bloody crewman she is holding and walks toward Dawn.

"Where is Shon?" The Queen demands.

"If you mean The Reaper, we killed him on Mars," Bragg answers from behind her. "Don't you remember?"

The Queen seems to calm down some. She stares at her blood-covered hands, and then looks around at the carnage she caused. The Queen frowns, seemingly bothered by what she has done. "What's wrong with me?" she mutters.

"You are just confused," Dawn says softly.

"My head is all messed up," The Queen replies, looking up at Dawn like a wounded animal.

"We will help you. We are friends, whether you want to admit it or not," Bragg says.

"Everything will be okay," Dawn pleads with The Queen.

"No. Not tis time," The Queen says. She is skittish, darting her eyes around the deck.

Dawn bends slightly, approaching The Queen gently. She holds her hands out in front of her in an attempt to appear as non-threatening as possible.

Just as Dawn reaches out to touch her hand, The Queen snatches it away. She starts to grow irate again. A huge vein bulges from her forehead. The Queen turns and sprints across the deck, and then enters the stolen ammo carrier.

Wait . . .

The hangar deck alarms blare. Lights flicker, signaling the opening of the exit doors.

"No, Shea! Don't!" Dawn yells.

Dawn sprints toward the carrier. She continues to chase it as it rockets down the runway, until it disappears into space.

The surviving Villains begin to stir. Most have a shell-shocked look, hovering over the dead and crying.

Bragg walks over to Dawn. "I'll bring her back," he says.

"I'm coming with you," Dawn says.

"No. I need you to stay here."

"I'm worried about you. You have been different lately."

"Don't worry. I'll be back soon."

24. Stellar Run
"Best you go home now."

Bragg is not okay. The effects of his torture become more prevalent with each passing day. Every time he blinks, he sees flickers of the spinning coin. Screams fill his head constantly. He cannot sleep for fear of dreaming of the sterile room. His exhaustion gives reality a haze.

He finds himself on the brink of madness.

MINERVA tracks The Queen's flight path to Stellar Run, a depressing colony located on Ceres. The entire asteroid has been encased in a bio dome, which provides an artificial atmosphere. The colony is constantly cold, making the destination look like a snow globe from afar. The colony is completely industrial, composed of several small towns populated by working-class miners who extract the asteroid's minerals and ship them back to Mars and Earth.

Bragg pursues The Queen. The Mark IX descends into the biodome's atmosphere, encountering a heavy snowstorm. The canopy shifts to infrared, replacing the cloudy view with rich colors that outline the landscape.

From the air, Bragg spots the crashed carrier burning at the bottom of a deep impact crater. The Mark IX's tractor beam lowers Bragg from the cockpit. His boots sink into the deep snow. The frigid wind stings his exposed skin. His insulated suit struggles to keep up with the temperature.

The carrier smolders on the side of a mountain trail, too damaged to fly. The Queen is nowhere in sight. Bragg discovers footprints in the snow leading from the crater. He follows the imprints down the trail.

The path runs through a heavily wooded area. The huge trunks of fir trees extend upwards, branches intertwined, only allowing sparse rays of sunlight through its canopy.

His WristTop shows the temperature is twenty-eight degrees Fahrenheit. His fingertips ache. His feet are numb. Bragg is unsure how far he can travel in these conditions.

The footprints end. The Queen's trail grows as cold as the temperature. The path leads down the mountain and all the way to a modest town. There are only a few streets. All the buildings are single story. Stop signs are used instead of traffic signals. No one is out in the weather.

Bragg enters a corner convenience store.

An alien clerk, with blue skin and black, insect-like eyes, looks up from a tablet. She greets Bragg from behind the front counter, in a language he does not recognize.

Bragg is the only customer. The store is surprisingly clean, with aisles of snacks and coolers on each wall containing cold drinks. Bragg walks to the back of the store and reaches into the cooler for a glass bottle of water.

Once he turns around, Bragg finds The Queen standing and staring at him menacingly at the end of the aisle of chip bags. She is still wearing the black one piece from the rehab chamber, drenched in slime and blood.

The bottle falls from Bragg's hand and shatters on the floor.

The Queen is breathing heavily. Behind her eyes lies nothing. Her skin is paler than usual.

Bragg looks past The Queen, at the alien clerk, who is behind the register shaking.

"Best you go home now," Bragg says to her.

The girl starts for the door but The Queen darts in front of her, blocking her path. While The Queen has always been unpredictable, Bragg senses something different about her now. This time, something inside her is unhinged.

The Queen grabs the clerk and puts her in a choke hold. With the alien's head between her bicep and forearm, The Queen squeezes tight.

The girl lets out a screeching squeak and begins to cry.

The Queen compresses her hold more as the clerk struggles. "I don't think her shift is over, Bragg," The Queen says.

"This is between us. It has nothing to do with this teenager, Shea," Bragg says.

"Shea? Even yer disrespect me now!" The Queen snarls.

The Queen snaps the girl's neck with a swift motion. Her lifeless body collapses to the floor.

The move catches Bragg off guard. The sheer heartlessness is difficult to comprehend. His knees grow weak.

This can't be happening. Everywhere I go, violence finds me.

Bragg flies into a rage. He pulls one of his ray guns from inside his suit jacket and aimlessly squeezes the trigger. The last round hits The Queen in the right thigh.

The Queen lets out a shrieking yell and falls down onto all fours.

The new rounds work.

As Bragg approaches her, his edge lasts a split second.

The Queen reaches out and pulls his legs out from under him. She then picks up Bragg from the floor and tosses him across the convenience store. Packs of snacks spill onto the floor beneath him.

Lying in a pile of squished prepackaged pastries, Bragg tries to regain his composure. The Queen stands over him with blood smeared across her thigh. She is like a rabid beast, acting on pure instinct and preying on those weaker than she is.

"I'm going to kill yer," she says.

"It won't be easy," Bragg responds.

The Queen lets out her signature laugh. Madness fills her eyes. She is almost foaming at the mouth. She picks up Bragg and throws him through the storefront's plate glass window.

Bragg hits his head against the concrete when he lands outside. Blood drips from his mouth and nose as he feels himself losing consciousness.

The Queen's bare feet appear on the ground in front of his face.

Bragg doesn't look up at her. He just stares at her soles as they crush the shards of glass beneath them, unbothered.

Maybe it will be easy to kill me, after all.

Bragg awakens at the bottom of the crash crater, next to the smoldering carrier. It is nightfall. His WristTop is busted. His hands are tied behind his back with rope. The knot is so tight it cuts into his flesh. He tries not to make it worse by moving, but the wintry air causes him to shiver.

The Queen sits a few feet in front of him, stoking a fire she built. Stellar Run's starry sky blankets them above. Bragg is grateful for the fire. His pants are wet from the snow-covered ground. His tattered suit hardly provides protection from the cold.

"Did yer know I was raised in an orphanage," The Queen says in a low voice, without looking up from the fire.

"Franklin mentioned it," Bragg replies. He sits up, hoping this may be a moment of clarity for The Queen.

"The human kids bullied me the entire time. So did the staff. Fer looking and sounding different. There I learned the cruelness of yer race," The Queen hisses. "When I turned sixteen, I fought my way out of the orphanage and joined The Villains. Franklin let me be my true self. He taught me to use my thirst fer killing in a productive way."

"So, all humans aren't bad? Not Franklin? Not The Villains?" Bragg asks.

"Where did yer git yer fancy ammo from?" she asks, completely ignoring his question.

Although it won't help his efforts, Bragg decides to be honest. "MINERVA helped me lace the rounds with yasphite, the material from The Prophets' pronged weapon."

"So, yer were planning to kill me?" The Queen asks.

"No. It was a precaution," Bragg replies.

"Yer fabricated strength has failed. And yer will pay fer yer mistake."

"Why kill me? Why kill any of The Villains?" Bragg asks.

"I DON'T KNOW!" The Queen screams so loudly it echoes through the woods.

What does she mean?

Of all the circumstances that could have exited Bragg from the world of the living, he finds this one the oddest. Her answer only invokes more questions. "I'm not your enemy. Come home and let us help you," he pleads.

"Shut up," The Queen says.

"Dawn waited for you to wake up. She never lost hope for a second."

"SHUT UP!" The Queen yells. She stands from the fire and approaches Bragg. She brings her hand back, readying to slap him.

Bragg looks into her eyes, unflinching. For a moment he can see through the blinding rage that has overcome her.

She lowers her hand and returns to the fire. "Yer humans will die. I will hunt yer to extinction," The Queen growls.

What is she talking about?

The night drags on. Bragg forces himself to stay awake. He tries to loosen The Queen's knot, moving his hands back and forth. The rope has rubbed his wrist so raw; it feels like sandpaper grinding the wound. Eventually, Bragg's body gives out and he falls asleep.

Dawn sloshes through wet snow the following day, moving towards the smoke plume in the distance. Her purple hair is in pigtails and she wears bulky Union military armor she found on the hangar deck. She checks the map displayed on her WristTop, showing she is approaching Bragg's location. Dawn can hear The Queen's laughter eerily bouncing around the towering trees, as if she is everywhere at once.

When she arrives at the source of the smoke, Dawn finds Bragg alone at the bottom of a crater. He is tied up next to the crashed carrier and not moving.

Dawn slides down the crater wall. She cuts the rope from his hands as Bragg starts to wake up.

Thank goodness he is alive!

"Are you hurt?" Dawn asks.

"I told you to stay on *The Spectator*," Bragg says, in a gravelly voice.

"Good thing I don't listen! You are welcome," Dawn replies.

"The Queen is mad. I can't get through to her," Bragg says. "We are in danger."

Dawn and Bragg emerge from the crater. The mountain trail overlooking Stellar Run provides a scenic view.

Bragg limps through the snow alongside Dawn. Dried blood and bruises cover his body. His blue suit is soiled and missing one sleeve. "I have rounds in my ray gun that can wound The Queen, but I dropped one when she attacked me," Bragg explains.

"You mean this ray gun?"

Dawn reaches behind her back and removes Bragg's coveted twin ray gun. She explains he dropped it "in some store." Aware they may need the specially crafted rounds before confronting The Queen, MINERVA advised Dawn to retrieve the weapon.

"Shea is different. She killed a store clerk for nothing," Bragg says as he takes the ray gun from Dawn.

"I THINK I MAY KNOW WHAT HAS HAPPENED TO SHEA, BUT IT IS JUST A THEORY," MINERVA chimes, from Dawn's WristTop.

Before MINERVA can explain further, The Queen drops down from a tree branch. She tackles Dawn and sends her tumbling off the side of the trail, down a steep slope.

Dawn collides with rocks and rough terrain below. Breath is knocked from her lungs. Painful jolts surge through her spine. Deep cuts lacerate her skin. She rolls a bit further before coming to a rest on her back, facing the sky.

The pain is excruciating, but Dawn cannot yell. She cannot move. The clouds gently drop snow on her face. She struggles and turns to look back up the cliff from which she fell. The fall looks treacherous.

Bragg must think I'm dead.

The Queen's voice startles Dawn from behind. "Alive, eh?"

Dawn tries again, but cannot move her arms or legs. Her back is glued to the thick snow.

The Queen appears, standing over Dawn, surrounded by powdery snowflakes being tossed around in the wind. "Yer rely on weak human tools. Body armor. Rey guns. They are no match fer true strength."

Dawn struggles to speak. "Why . . . why are you trying to kill me?"

The Queen turns and walks away. "Yer know, I really cared fer yer. Tell me yer didn't feel the same?"

Dawn grunts as she regains feeling in her toes and fingers. She coughs blood as she pushes down on the snow. With great agony, Dawn manages to stand on her shaky legs. She looks to her left, finding another drop off. Alone and unarmed, the situation looks unfavorable.

"I'll always care for you. We just aren't good together," Dawn replies in a raspy voice.

She barely manages to stay conscious, swaying on her feet.

"Look at how tough yer are," The Queen says, standing a few yards away now. "That's what I always liked about yer."

"Then why . . . are . . . you trying to kill me?" Dawn asks.

The Queen drops her head. When she raises it again, her eyes are on fire. "Because in the end, yer the weaker race. I have to destroy yer with the rest of them."

In the blink of an eye, The Queen grabs Dawn by the throat and lifts her off the ground. She chokes Dawn with chilly, pale hands.

Dawn tries to claw the grip away, but it is no use. Dawn's feet dangle in desperation. She gasps for air and starts to black out.

Suddenly The Queen lets out a scream and drops Dawn.

Tears fill Dawn's eyes, making her vision blurry. A nasty fit of coughing plagues her.

Once Dawn can see, she notices The Queen has dropped to one knee. She is bleeding profusely from two holes in her abdomen. Behind The Queen, Dawn can see Bragg holding his ray gun. The muzzle is smoking.

"Are you okay?" he yells.

"Yes."

Bragg fires again, but his rounds miss. Even with her wounds, The Queen can move evasively enough.

Frenzied, she closes in on Bragg. The Queen snatches up Bragg, holding him above her head with both hands like a competition trophy.

Dread floods through Dawn as The Queen begins to walk toward the drop off.

"Tis is it, Dawn! Time to say goodbye to yer boyfriend," The Queen says.

Dawn stumbles toward them with all her might. She is pleading for The Queen to stop.

Her requests fall on deaf ears. The Queen heaves Bragg off the mountainside.

They are so high, the ground can't be seen. Dawn arrives just in time to see Bragg disappear beneath the clouds.

Dawn screams so loud it ricochets off the mountain, broadcasting her suffering to the entire asteroid. She wants to follow him down. After all the times he has saved her from certain death, Dawn finds herself failing Bragg.

He is gone. Bragg is really gone.

"Don't fret. Yer'll be . . . joining him soon," The Queen taunts. But she drops to both knees. Her voice trails off. Her breath becomes labored. Blood gushes from her abdomen. Her wounds don't appear to be recovering at their normal rate.

Dawn finds Bragg's ray gun lying in the snow a few feet away. She checks the cartridge and finds there is one round left. It whines as Dawn cocks it. She limps over to The Queen, who is now the one lying motionless in the snow.

Dawn glares down into The Queen's eyes. "You heartless bitch!"

"I'm glad it's yer. I want it to be yer that ends it," The Queen says.

Dawn's hand shakes as she tries to steady the barrel of the ray gun. Without another word, Dawn pulls the trigger.

The Queen's long existence has come to an end.

I've lost everybody.

The mountainside begins to shake. Trees sway so hard they look like they could topple over. A familiar Union fighter rises from the drop off. Through the Mark IX's canopy Dawn can see Bragg, sitting there unconscious. Her heart skips a beat.

"I WAS ABLE TO CATCH HIM," MINERVA says from Dawn's WristTop. ***"BUT HE NEEDS MEDICAL."***

The tractor beam pulls Dawn into the cockpit. The Mark IX then rockets toward *The Spectator*.

"Why did The Queen do this?" Dawn asks.

MINERVA speaks from the cockpit's speakers. *"SHEA'S ALIEN RACE, THE VAMPREX, ARE FROM THE ALPHA CENTAURI SYSTEM. ALTHOUGH THEY LIVE HUNDREDS OF YEARS, WHEN THEY NEAR THE END OF THEIR LIFE CYCLE THEY SLOWLY GO INSANE AND BECOME MORE AGGRESSIVE. SHEA WAS FAR TOO YOUNG TO HAVE THE CONDITION I SPEAK OF; HOWEVER MY THEORY IS THE REHABILITATION CHAMBER CAUSED AN EARLY ONSET OF THE SYMPTOMS."*

"Was there any way to treat her?" Dawn asks.

"NO."

Dawn wonders if that is the truth, or another one of MINERVA's irrational lies.

25. War and Peace
"The Queen is Dead."

When Bragg awakens, he finds himself in the medical bay of *The Spectator*. As soon as he tries to remember how he got there, he recalls a sense of falling. He springs up in the bed, only to be calmed by Dawn's soothing voice.

"Easy. Everything is fine now," Dawn says.

"Sorry, I have this thing about . . ."

"Being woken up. I know," Dawn replies with a gentle smile. "You've been in the rehab chamber for three days."

Three days?

Dawn sits close to the right side of the bed. Her face is swollen and bruised. There is a scabbed gash from her left cheek to her upper lip. The entire sclera of her left eye is blood red.

"Where is The Queen?" Bragg asks.

"The Queen is dead," Dawn explains. "MINERVA discovered the rehab chamber drove Shea insane." Tears streak down her cheeks.

Bragg reaches out and softly grabs her hand. He also feels the sorrow of The Queen's death, especially now that he knows the underlying cause.

She wasn't so bad.

"I'm going to miss her," Bragg admits.

"Shea didn't get sick on purpose, you know? She was loyal to Franklin and The Villains for a long time before we came along," Dawn says. "I just want to keep her legacy intact."

"We will," Bragg promises.

We will keep all their legacies intact.

MINERVA interrupts from the speakers above. ***"COMMANDER. I HAVE RE-ESTABLISHED CONTACT WITH THE UNION'S NETWORK. THE SITUATION IS NOT WHAT WE EXPECTED."***

"What do you mean?" Bragg asks.

"A GROUP HAS DISCLOSED UNION SECRETS ON SPACE-WIDE MEDIA. MANY IN THE SPACE FORCE HAVE DESERTED. A REBELLION SEEMS TO HAVE STARTED. CITIZENS ON EARTH HAVE BEGUN TO REVOLT ACROSS THE PLANET."

"Shit. We might have a shot at this yet," Dawn states.

"I HAVE ALSO MADE CONTACT WITH IMANI."

"Put it through," Bragg says.

After brief static, Imani's voice blasts through the overhead speakers. *"Bragg?"* Imani asks.

"Yes. What happened?"

"Shit has gone crazy! Union soldiers are attacking Meridian. We can hardly hold them off. They are killing everyone – women, kids, it doesn't matter!"

"Are you with other Villains?" Bragg asks.

"Around twenty. And some of the deserters have joined. Rumor is an entire Union destroyer crew has rebelled."

"We are on our way. There is just one stop we have to make," Bragg says.

During Bragg's time with the Union, he went to the Lunar Penal Colony twice. Once to fly in supplies and again to transport prisoners of war. Both visits provided the insight needed to get The Villains through the security.

The Lunar Colony is an impenetrable fortress. Beneath the surface, the Moon has been hollowed out and converted into narrow corridors and holding cells. Satellites surrounding the Moon are linked to create a protective force field that keeps prisoners in and everyone else out. Countless floating turrets orbit the force field, armed with lasers strong enough to tear ships like *The Spectator* to shreds.

Every time a ship approaches the force field, it must get clearance to enter through an opening that changes every hour. Without clearance, it is nearly impossible to determine where access to the Colony lies.

The Spectator waits, hidden in the debris of a destroyed space station located roughly between Earth and Mars. With the running lights off and the visible damage from its previous fight, the warship looks disabled.

Bragg sits in the pilot's seat with his arms crossed, mentally rehearsing the plan.

Jasmine sits in the navigator's seat next to him.

Kora and Mathis man two of the posts behind them.

The crew are all at battle stations. The tension is palpable.

"Should it take this long?" Kora asks in a low whisper.

A nearby warp gate surges to life. A gash tears open in space. The bridge's view is partially obscured by the station debris. They watch as *The Revenant*, a command ship five times the size of *The Spectator*, emerges from warp space. The hull is oval shaped and painted sparkling white. Navy blue Union stripes are painted down the sides.

"REMEMBER, COMMANDER. I CAN ONLY MASK OUR SIGNAL FOR TEN SECONDS."

Bragg grips the control wheel. The window will be tight. "Keep running silent, MINERVA."

Just as the aft section of *The Revenant* passes, Bragg throttles up and brings *The Spectator* out of the debris. He flies directly behind the command ship. The bow of *The Spectator* is almost touching the rear thrusters of *The Revenant*. The front viewport is filled with flames. Red indicators on the dashboard flicker, signaling the strain on the forward shields.

"YOU ARE IN THE BLINDSPOT. REMAIN HERE."

With skill that astonishes the crew, Bragg tailgates the command ship for over an hour. There has been no indication that the Union is aware of The Villains. Flying in this reckless manner has kept *The Spectator* hidden from radar and from sight.

Eventually, MINERVA's voice comes through the bridge's speakers again. *"COMMANDER, WE ARE APPROACHING THE FORCE FIELD."*

Jasmine takes Bragg's place in the pilot's seat. He and Mathis take the elevator down to the hangar deck. When they arrive, Bragg finds Dawn standing with six other Villains around the egg-shaped carrier. She is wearing military armor that has been spray painted royal blue.

No way.

"Dawn, you must remain on *The Spectator*," Bragg tells her.

"Why do you say that every time? I can help!" Dawn replies.

"And you will. Here. You are in command while I'm gone."

"Me? I . . . are you sure?"

"I've already told the crew."

The Spectator shudders hard. Turrets from the Moon's surface begin to fire on the ship.

"We are through the force field," Bragg tells the other Villains aboard the carrier. "Keep our gun deck firing," he says to Dawn before jumping aboard the carrier and piloting it out into open space.

The fire fight between *The Spectator* and the Moon lights up the area. MINERVA pinpoints *The Revenant* trying to dock with the Lunar Colony.

Bragg sends the carrier into a dive, trying to head off the command ship. Only a few of the Moon's turrets target the carrier, allowing Bragg to avoid the incoming blasts.

The Moon focuses on fending off *The Spectator*. Without the aid of the floating turrets outside the force field, *The Spectator* is winning the battle for now.

Alarms sound throughout the passenger compartment of the carrier. The Villains aboard begin to protest as Bragg maintains his course.

Mathis signs something furiously, which Bragg interprets roughly as concern.

"They'll pull off first. This is our only chance to breach the Colony. Once the command ship is in, they will secure the port," Bragg tells the others aboard.

The carrier continues barreling toward the docking port. *The Revenant* does not change course. Bragg throttles up, but the carrier has no more to give.

Mathis grabs Bragg's shoulder.

"They'll pull off," Bragg repeats. This mission is all or nothing. There is no room for doubt.

Just as the carrier arrives at the port entrance, *The Revenant* raises its nose and avoids a collision with The Villains. The carrier screams through the force field and into the docking port.

Staff and guards flee for cover below as Bragg fires braking thrusters to halt the carrier. The bottom of the craft scrapes against the deck until the carrier slides to a stop.

"Stack up!" Bragg shouts to The Villains.

The Villains line up near the carrier's rear exit.

Screams fill the docking port outside.

"IMPLEMENTING INCAPACITATING GAS. STAND BY."

The yelling outside intensifies for a bit, before gradually ceasing.

"Move," Bragg says, as the rear of the carrier opens. He un-holsters his ray guns and surveys the area. All the guards in the docking bay, approximately thirty men, are laid out incapacitated.

"MINERVA. We are in," Bragg says into his WristTop.

"OPENING CORRIDOR B AND LOCKING THE OTHERS. THAT SHOULD REDUCE THEIR NUMBERS SIGNIFICANTLY."

A door at the end of the port opens. Bragg leads Mathis and the six other Villains down the dimly lit passage. It slopes downward, beneath the Moon's surface. The grimy walls seem to narrow the further they walk, squeezing them together. The air is stagnant.

As The Villains approach another door, it begins to rise, allowing them to pass. The next corridor has cells along both sides, so tiny the people held inside are forced to stand. Transparent force field doors hold the occupants prisoner. Their faces light up at the sight of The Villains and the inmates yell at them from their cells as they pass.

Bragg imagines the torment of being held inside one. His skin crawls at the thought. He considers death a better alternative.

"THE VILLAINS ARE HELD IN THE NEXT SECTION," MINERVA says. The entrance to the next corridor opens. ***"PREPARE YOURSELVES. ENEMIES AHEAD."***

"Get down," Bragg says.

The Villains take cover behind meal carts on the side of the corridor.

There are countless guards in body armor blocking the passage, ready to attack. Bragg calls out to them. "You can surrender now and walk away with your lives," he offers. But there is so much silence that Bragg grows concerned.

"Fuck you, traitor," a voice finally replies.

All right.

Mathis removes a grenade from his belt and tosses it.

The Villains all fall prone.

Just as the guards notice the tumbling explosive, it goes off and splatters them across the corridor. The surviving guards flee, allowing The Villains to rise from their cover.

"MINERVA, open them," Bragg says into his WristTop.

The lighting above flickers. The force field doors power down, releasing all The Villains from their cells. They gradually step into the corridor, all uniformed in olive green prison uniforms. Excitement spreads among the twenty or so men and women.

"I can't believe it," a stout Villain says. He is older and heavily tattooed, all the way up his neck.

"You don't have to believe it. Just follow us," Bragg urges.

The unified Villains return to the docking port. Dawn's voice comes through Bragg's WristTop. *"We have destroyed the Moon's turrets. But this command ship is hammering us. The Union has closed the force field.* The Spectator *is trapped within."*

"I CANNOT OVERRIDE IT," MINERVA adds. **"I DO NOT KNOW WHY."**

The Villains in the docking port stare at Bragg.

What now? Mathis signs.

Bragg is afraid to tell them the truth. He has no other plan. No more schemes. They have come close to their goal, but failed. The Union is going to win. Bragg can already feel the tiny cell closing in around him.

"The Spectator won't last much longer. We are going to fight to the end, but . . . it is not looking good," Dawn says through the voice channel.

"I should have never put you in this situation," Bragg replies.

"Stop it," she says. *"You have made my life – "*

A loud explosion drowns out Dawn's voice. The voice channel closes. Bragg frantically presses the touchscreen on his WristTop, trying to re-establish the connection. He cannot.

Bragg becomes numb. He feels like screaming.

I can't lose Dawn!

The voice channel roars back to life with static, this time with Kora on the other end. *"Bragg! The biggest Union ship I've ever seen is out here!"*

"Can you concentrate fire on it?" Bragg asks.

"No! You don't understand. It's . . . it's helping us, I think. The Union let it through the force field, but it started attacking the command ship!"

Helping us?

Bragg realizes he is wasting time trying to make sense of it. "We will thank them later. Dock *The Spectator*. We are getting out of here."

26. Utopia
"Maybe we shouldn't press our luck."

Bragg returns to the bridge of *The Spectator.*

Mathis and the older tattooed prisoner enter behind him.

Dawn stands up from the navigator's seat and gives Bragg a hug. Her warmth presses against him, relieving his anxiety.

Jasmine pilots *The Spectator* out of the docking port. She starts to relinquish the controls to Bragg, but he signals for her to stay.

The Spectator exits the Lunar Penal Colony, dwarfed by the Union destroyer. Its hull is long and angular, painted navy blue with white stripes. A tube-shaped plasma cannon runs the length of its undercarriage. Stubby wings encase two round ion engines on the sides.

The battered shell of *The Revenant* floats next to the destroyer. It is without power. Escape pods are sprinkled around the command ship's corpse.

The voice channel in *The Spectator's* bridge clicks on. *"This is Captain Elijah Lewis of* The Phoenix. *Respond."*

Eli?

Bragg recognizes the name and voice immediately. However, the Eli Lewis he once knew was an ensign.

"This is Samuel Bragg of *The Spectator.*"

"Commander! I knew it was you. You saved my life a few times. Figured I'd return the favor," Eli says.

"We are grateful. However, the Union will not be happy with you and your crew."

"We have joined the rebellion, Commander. The stuff they had us doing was . . ." Eli's voice trails off.

"They brainwashed us," Bragg finishes. He knows the guilt can be almost insurmountable.

"When this rebellion started, they gave me orders to bomb New Francisco from orbit. Half of my crew's family lives there. I just couldn't. We have to make it right, as best we can," Eli says. *"I have two hundred souls aboard. We are taking* The Phoenix *to Earth. Most of the fighting is around the Eastern hemisphere."*

"We must return to Meridian. Our allies need help."

"The Union is killing everyone who does not comply with their demands. Be careful."

"You, too, Eli." The voice channel clicks off. "Dawn, plot a course to Earth."

"Maybe we shouldn't press our luck," Jasmine says. "We rescued The Villains from the penal colony. Those on Earth are a lost cause. Let's just go to Europa now."

"Franklin would not have us leave our comrades behind," Bragg says boldly. He hopes the name drop will quell this revolt.

"Franklin is dead," Jasmine replies.

"Watch your fucking mouth!" Dawn shouts.

Before Bragg can interject, the prisoner speaks up from behind them. "Do we get a vote? We are looking for a chance to get back at the Union."

"You think everyone from the penal colony feels that way?" Bragg asks. "You haven't even been free for an hour."

"On the inside, I kept us together," the prisoner says. "I know them."

"Who are you?" Jasmine asks, looking back.

"Wade," the prisoner responds.

"Franklin used to talk about you," Dawn adds.

"He and I were close," Wade says.

"I'm sorry," Dawn says.

"Don't be, beautiful. Franklin got more good years out of this life than most," Wade says.

"We have to help Meridian," Bragg says. "We wouldn't just be leaving our own, but abandoning a city that has been great to us."

"Then let's go home," Dawn says.

The Mark IX descends through the milky clouds of Earth's troposphere. Bragg slows his breathing, focusing on the soft chimes and beeps bouncing around the cockpit. He clears his mind, preparing to take on the task ahead.

Jasmine pilots the egg-shaped carrier behind him, jammed to capacity with ten Villains. If they manage to land in Meridian, the plan is for her to drop off the passengers and return to *The Spectator* to pick up more.

Once Bragg is through the clouds, he cannot believe his eyes. A Union heavy bomber strafes the metro with ordinance. Plumes of smoke smolder up from the city. The skyscrapers are zombies of their former selves, leaning haphazardly and missing entire sections.

Bragg banks away from the carrier and flies lower to get a better view. The streets are filled with citizens fighting to the death with Union soldiers. Meridian is consumed by mayhem.

"MINERVA. Find a place for Jasmine to set the carrier down. Wade, you guys get to Imani," Bragg says through the voice channel.

He pulls back on the control stick, forcing the Mark IX to climb. Scanning the horizon, he spots the heavy bomber and throttles after it. *Regaining air superiority will help.*

The wingspan of the bomber is massive. It casts an ominous shadow over Meridian as it rains destruction. As the Mark IX approaches, a sphere at the rear of the bomber swivels toward Bragg. Twin barrels extending from the sphere open fire, peppering the Mark IX's shields with laser rounds.

Bragg moves the control stick side to side, activating the side thrusters, swimming the fighter like a fish through the air. This makes him a more difficult target and allows the shields to take less damage.

Firing his guns within Earth's atmosphere will decelerate the Mark IX, so Bragg refrains. He boosts power to his forward shields and focuses on closing the distance. Although Bragg manages to dodge most of the oncoming fire, the rounds that connect chip away at his defenses.

"FORWARD SHIELDS ARE AT SEVENTY PERCENT. SIXTY PERCENT. FORTY PERCENT," MINERVA warns.

Bragg takes another deep breath. His finger hovers over the trigger.

Closer. Closer.

"SHIELDS ARE AT TWENTY-FIVE PERCENT."

An instinctual pull of the trigger sends streaks of red laser bolts through the bomber. Bragg is so close the rounds drain the enemy's shields instantly. A few seconds pass before it explodes in a thunderous ball of fire.

"Bomber's down," Bragg says into the voice channel.

"We can see that," Wade's voice replies. *"Nice work, space cadet. We found Imani and the others. They are holed up in this old diner. The owner said you'd know the one."*

"Indeed," Bragg responds, veering the fighter off toward Highland Street.

Jasmine's voice cuts in. *"I'm almost back to* The Spectator. *I passed some Union fighters on their way to Meridian. I need them to stay away from the carrier as I bring reinforcements."*

The cockpit lights up red from warnings. The canopy circles eight Mark X fighters approaching from ahead.

The voice channel crackles with static, then clicks on. *"Time to prove who is the best! Who is going to take down the legend!"* a pilot taunts.

Bragg ignores the message.

The Mark Xs have a more modern design, with a narrow cone-shaped nose and short wings that point downward. A rudder stands tall behind the cockpit, above three tubular boosters at the rear. Their navy-blue paint is accented by gold on the nose.

One of the red circles on the canopy glows, signaling a Mark X is preparing to fire. A bright green beam streaks through the sky. By the time it reaches Bragg, the round is far off target to his left.

Bragg uses the side boosters to strafe the Mark IX. Deadly green beams continue to dart past the canopy, forcing Bragg to fly erratically to avoid the oncoming destruction.

Okay, how about this?

Bragg flies directly at the enemy's V-shaped formation, barreling toward the fighters at full throttle. He gets so close to the formation it disperses.

The enemy is now flying aimlessly. Bragg maneuvers behind one of the fighters and closes the gap between them within seconds. Bragg refrains from squeezing the trigger on his control stick until his reticle has a lock on the area between the enemy's booster and right wing. He finally fires, sending the fighter into a controlled dive.

The cockpit glows red, signaling an enemy has a lock on him. Bragg shimmies the control stick, causing the cockpit light to flicker. Most pilots won't fire with a shaky target lock.

On the screen to the left of the control stick, Bragg can see the enemy fighter that has zeroed onto his rear.

Must be a trainee. He is too close.

Bragg throttles his fighter completely down, still twitching the control stick. The Mark X continues past Bragg until he is ahead of his reticle. Without hesitation Bragg fires the Mark IX's guns, destroying the enemy.

Six more to go.

It takes Bragg a little over five minutes to disable the rest of the enemy, leaving their escape pods floating in the air by parachutes. The Mark IX takes no damage.

Just as Bragg begins to relax, the cockpit glows red again. Another squadron approaches. This one is tougher than the last, but not enough to best Bragg. The Mark IX zips in and out of the enemy's formation and one by one he destroys the more veteran pilots.

The Union sends two squadrons next. Sixteen fighters. They fly in a formation Bragg is unfamiliar with, staggered and spread out. As the Mark IX floats idly outside their range of fire, Bragg riles himself up and lets out a yell that fills the cockpit. "You want more? You'll get more!"

"WAIT COMMANDER! YOUR WEAPON ENERGY –"

He throttles up and charges toward the enemy. Then he squeezes the control stick's trigger.

Nothing happens.

My guns are drained.

"Bragg, I'm returning for the last group now! Almost done!" Jasmine yells, through the voice channel.

They need more time. Before Bragg can react, enemy laser rounds strike the Mark IX in the right wing.

Alarms sound in the cockpit. Pulling the control stick hard, Bragg pivots his fighter and plots a course back to *The Spectator*.

The Mark Xs pursue him.

Dawn checks her body armor and rifle. She is in the hangar bay of *The Spectator*, surrounded by prisoners freed from the Lunar Penal Colony. Each is dressed in their green inmate uniform.

The egg-shaped carrier zooms through the force field at the end of the runway. It pivots and lands gently. The back opens and the ramp lowers to the deck. The Villains load into the carrier, as if they have done this a hundred times before.

Dawn climbs aboard last and tries to stand farthest in the back.

Jasmine turns around in the pilot seat and notices her immediately.   "Bragg said you are to stay aboard *The Spectator*," Jasmine protests.

"He means well, but he is wrong," Dawn replies. "The Villains down there need all the help they can get."

To Dawn's surprise, the reunited Villains voice support for her decision.

"Hell, yeah!" one of The Villains shouts, from the front.

"Fuck it. Let her fight," the Villain standing next to Dawn says. He winks and blows a kiss at her.

Jasmine puts up no more resistance. She swivels forward and presses a button on the console. The rear door closes. The carrier leaves the hangar deck and heads to Meridian.

As The Villains approach Earth, Dawn can see flashes of a firefight in the distance. The carrier zips past multiple enemy fighters pursuing the Mark IX in the opposite direction. She can see that Bragg is heading back toward *The Spectator*.

"What is going on?" Dawn asks MINERVA, through her WristTop.

"BRAGG APPEARS TO BE OUT OF WEAPON ENERGY."

"Wait – what??" Dawn asks, panicked.

"DO NOT WORRY. THE COMMANDER WILL BE FINE. STAY FOCUSED."

Once they enter the atmosphere, the scene saddens Dawn. Meridian is in ruin.

Are we too late?

The carrier lands three blocks away from Bryan and Keisha's diner. The Villains exit to mayhem. The city is a war zone. The streets are crowded with civilians fighting soldiers. Their makeshift weapons are little match against the riot gear. There are laser rounds firing in all directions, forcing The Villains to take cover behind the crumbled walls of what used to be a clinic. They stay low and move swiftly toward the diner.

Dawn grips the rifle, eyes darting around at the surrounding carnage. Storefront windows are shattered. Hover vehicles are aflame in the streets.

The former inmates form a semi-circle around Dawn, shooting any soldiers brave enough to attack. The group of Villains manages to make it to the diner without any losses.

Inside, Dawn finds the diner full of shell-shocked Villains. Bryan and Keisha are behind the counter talking with Imani. As soon as she spots Dawn, Imani frowns and steps away from the couple midsentence. "Dawn, what are you doing here?"

"Fighting for our survival. What else?"

"Bragg wouldn't want you getting hurt," Imani says.

"Then I won't get hurt," Dawn says.

The Villains split up. Some frantically search Meridian for citizens and bring them back. The remaining Villains stay behind to fortify the storefronts around the block.

Kora and Mathis are finishing up with the diner. Wood planks are secured over the plate glass windows. A tall, sturdy wooden shelf blocks the back door, sealing it. The diner is dusky. Beams of sunshine peek through cracks between the planks.

Dawn is sitting in a corner booth of the diner. Her hands shake as she loads laser rounds into her rifle. As the ammo clicks into place, Dawn worries about Bragg.

Is he okay?

With defiant looks on their wrinkled faces, Bryan and Keisha stand next to each other behind the counter. In their hands are laser shotguns that dwarf them in size.

Mathis secures the front door with one last piece of wood.

Imani's voice comes through the voice channel. *"We have most of the civilians secured in the storefronts on the end of the street. Union troopers were right behind us, so it won't be long."*

Sporadic laser rounds riddle the diner. They blast holes through the wood barricades and shatter all the glass.

Dawn dives from the booth. Debris showers her as she crawls. She takes cover behind the main counter next to Kora and the elderly couple.

The laser rounds cease, replaced with an eerie silence. She can hear someone forcing their way in, followed by the crunching of glass and heavy footsteps on the other side of the counter.

Next to Dawn, Kora reaches underneath her blue puffer jacket and removes a laser pistol. She peeks over the counter cautiously.

Dawn covers her mouth to conceal the sound of her erratic breathing.

Kora motions the count of three.

Dawn readies the rifle.

I can do this. I have to.

She takes a deep, satisfying breath, and then musters the courage to spring up from behind the counter.

Men in riot gear stare at her with the look of hunters realizing they are hunted.

A squeeze of the trigger nearly jolts Dawn's arm out of its socket. A few more squeezes follow. The rifle sends rounds through the men, almost cutting them in half.

Brilliant blue bolts soar from the muzzle of Kora's laser pistol. They sail through the diner with reasonable accuracy, collapsing every soldier they meet. The air becomes warm from their energy.

The other Villains emerge from hiding and join in. The remaining soldiers begin to flee, desperately trying to escape the onslaught.

Once the store appears clear of the intruders, a deafening buzzing noise fills the air. Mathis walks over towards a hole in one of the window's planks. After peeking out and investigating, he turns and signs frantically.

"Get down!" Kora yells. "Tank!"

The diner feels like it is being bulldozed. The foundation shakes so hard that pieces of the ceiling crack. Gigantic laser beams flare through the storefront window and continue to strike the diner, setting it ablaze and filling the area with billowy smoke.

"Get up!" Dawn yells, shielding Bryan and Keisha with her body. Dawn helps Keisha to her feet, holding her so she keeps her head down as they move.

Mathis gets to the back door first, pushing the bulky shelf away and kicking the door open. The group makes their way down the alley behind the diner.

Flames begin to engulf the outside of the building. The tank's cannon is still going off in the background, echoing like sinister thunder. Dawn's ears are ringing as she helps Keisha walk.

When the group emerges from the alleyway, a mob of twenty or thirty civilians are standing in the middle of the street. All of them are holding firearms. Aside from the mob, the street and the sidewalk are completely deserted.

Howard, the tailor, steps forward from the crowd. "I told them to stay hidden, but they wanted to help. I gave them proper weapons."

"We appreciate you all. More than you know. However, they are much too tough," Keisha says to the crowd, stepping away from Dawn.

In the street, it's quiet. The thunderous cannon in the background has ceased. But more alarming is the fact that it has been stopped for some time. Just as Dawn brings this to the attention of the others, the hover tank rounds the corner at the end of the street.

Its grill is lined with bars that resemble menacing teeth. Atop the tank sits a cannon the size of a sedan. The six-foot-long barrel swivels around. A plated housing unit protects someone behind the cannon's trigger. Beady white eyes peer through the narrow-armored viewport.

Marching around the tank, in formation, are rows of soldiers dressed in black riot gear. Each holds a laser rifle against his or her chest.

The synchronicity of their boots are like drums of impending doom.

Fucking monsters.

The civilians start to shriek and recoil, but no one flees. Dawn stands in front of the crowd and aims her rifle at the approaching tank. Kora steps up next to Dawn. Then Mathis. Gradually, all of The Villains shield the citizens of Meridian.

This is one hell of a way to go out.

Suddenly the clouds in the distance part. The Mark IX buzzes past above, strafing the tank with what feels like a hundred rounds from its twin guns.

The tank explodes, setting most of the surrounding soldiers aflame. The fighter ascends back into the clouds with poetic grace.

"It's Bragg!" cries Dawn. "Let's get them!"

Dawn leads the mob of shop owners. They take off in a mad race down the street, waving their firearms. Once the remaining ten or fifteen shell-shocked soldiers notice the charging crowd, most of them retreat.

When the carnage is over, the shop owners cheer in the street. They hug each other and throw things into the air. They sing praises to The Villains with their hands outstretched to the sky.

Dawn is exhausted. She follows The Villains through the crowd. People hug Dawn and pat her on the back. Tears well up in their eyes. She cannot remember someone being so grateful.

The rebellion rages on for six more grueling months. The Villains on the ground defend Meridian and the surrounding area from the Union. The Villains in space use *The Spectator* to aid the rebels in orbit until, eventually, the Third Interplanetary War is won. After suffering massive losses, the Union agrees to a cease fire.

Union President Teresa Howard negotiates with Elijah Lewis, captain of *The Phoenix* and interim President of Earth. After days of talks, news finally reaches The Villains aboard *The Spectator*: The Union has agreed to release Earth from its jurisdiction, allowing the planet and the Lunar Colony to be sovereign. Mars and the Asteroid Belt will remain in the Union. Since Earth and Mars are co-dependent, trade will continue pursuant to contracts that shall be renegotiated every four Earth calendar years.

However, the agreement also entails a term that is outright rejected by The Villains and the citizens of Meridian. "The disgraced

Commander Samuel Bragg shall be surrendered to the Union."

Despite Bragg insisting he surrender himself for the overall interests of the planet, The Villains decide to counter with another proposal. Samuel Bragg will leave both Earth and Union occupied space for good. The Villains also vow to depart with their revered commander, and to venture to Europa.

The Union accepts the counter.

The gang returns to Meridian and finds a hero's welcome waiting for them. Their celebrity status is amplified tenfold. The Villains are planetary legends, known as "the group that bested the Union." Each Villains' headshot is mounted around the walls of city hall.

Meridian and Comet City are united, now named Utopia. All the citizens seem to do something to support The Villains. A local cult donates ten crates of non-perishable food. A company volunteers to paint and reinforce the hull of *The Spectator*. Drinks are comped for an entire week for the gang at every open establishment.

Imani is elected mayor by the Utopian citizens, after Dawn and Bragg decline their nominations.

Credits are donated. Public utilities are improved. Construction of a police station, a fire department, and a better school are all started.

Everyone beams with pride when they say they are from the home of the infamous Villains. A statue of Franklin Hendrix is erected in the center of the city. He would be proud to see it all.

The Villains freed from the Lunar Penal Colony choose to remain in Utopia, renouncing their membership in the gang to abide by the peace treaty. They promise to help rebuild and protect the city in case the Union attacks.

President Lewis and The Phoenix patrol Earth's orbit, acting as the planetary vanguard.

Alone, Dawn sits in Bryan and Keisha's diner. The couple has kindly locked the door to stop the press from bombarding Dawn while she eats. A spread of pancakes, synthetic sausage, and grapes sits before her.

Keisha comes over to the booth and refills Dawn's coffee. "How do you feel about leaving, dear?" Keisha asks.

"A fair mix of excitement and fear," Dawn replies.

"I wish I could go with you. You are going to see things humanity is not meant to see," Keisha says.

"You could come with us. Both you and Bryan," Dawn says, staring down into the black coffee.

"Bryan and I are much too old for adventure, dear. Besides, we are the official hangout of the legendary Villains. Business is booming," Keisha replies.

Dawn laughs, slightly choking on a bite of the pancakes.

27. Uncharted Space
"We have never met. However, you know me well. Good luck."

The Spectator's fifteen other crewmen are gathered on the hangar deck.

On the bridge, Jasmine pilots the warship as Bragg sits next to her in the navigator's seat. Dawn is standing over Bragg's shoulder, gripping it tensely. His heart is in his throat as he leads his group, his family, into the unknown.

The Spectator exits the last of the Asteroid Belt. MINERVA has pinpointed the coordinates to the last warp gate, tracking it on the bridge's center display and above the hangar deck simultaneously so everyone can see. All eyes are glued to the projections. No one talks. The triangle icon representing *The Spectator* inches past the green gridlines, into uncharted space.

Jasmine clears her throat, finally breaking the silence that has plagued the bridge. "My memaw told me that monsters live on Europa. That they hate humans and eat whoever dares to look for them."

"Now you tell us," Dawn replies.

"I heard Jupiter doesn't even have a moon. The whole thing is a myth," Kora says from the seat behind them.

"That's dumb. It's basic science. Jupiter has a moon. It's just supposedly uninhabitable," Dawn says.

"There are beings that live there. They just aren't smart like humans," adds Jasmine.

Bragg does not bother to correct them. Europa definitely exists. And someone, or something, is there.

"Shut up, everybody! We are here," Jasmine says.

There is nothing. The triangle is right over the coordinate on the projection. But there is just space.

Bragg double checks *The Spectator's* scans. Nothing shows on the readouts. Infrared, sonar, everything; it's all quiet.

Where is the warp gate? What if there is no warp gate?

The bridge is silent once more. Disappointment begins to fill the room, suffocating all the occupants.

"STAND BY," MINERVA says from above.

Tiny blue lights appear in front of *The Spectator's* bow, dotted in a circle.

Bragg checks the ship's sensor. Again, nothing shows.

The blue dots begin to rotate along the circle, increasing in pace until they blur together.

The Spectator moves forward toward the gate.

"Jasmine, wait. Let's see what happens," Bragg says.

"It's not me!" she says, sounding a little frantic.

"MINERVA. Halt the ship," Bragg commands.

"I CANNOT, COMMANDER. THE GATE IS PULLING US IN."

Unlike normal warp tunnels, *The Spectator* is surrounded by milky white walls so bright they hurt Bragg's eyes. Time slows substantially. Bragg has the sense he is floating, and peace overwhelms him. All his worry evaporates.

The Spectator exits warp. The sight outside the viewport is almost inconceivable. Even at a safe distance, Jupiter's sheer size is intimidating. Its atmosphere is violent with sandy brown bands fighting blue swirls.

The environment defies science. The gravitational pull from the planet's mass should be devouring *The Spectator*. However, everything is eerily calm.

"This is incredible," Dawn mumbles.

Jasmine leans over to Bragg. "Commander, will you take the helm?"

As Bragg trades seats with Jasmine, MINERVA comes through the overhead speakers. ***"NEW WAYPOINT DISPLAYED. EUROPA."***

Another waypoint appears on the navigation screen.

Once the moon comes into view, The Villains erupt in celebration. Compared to its host planet, Europa is a marble. Red lines are scribbled all over the surface as if drawn on by a child.

Dawn jumps in Bragg's lap, face to face with him. She hugs him tight and kisses him with more passion than ever before.

The Villains begin to chant *Bragg! Bragg!*

Bragg is overcome with emotion.

And then, just like that, Bragg is somewhere else. He is no longer aboard *The Spectator*. No longer in space.

Bragg finds himself lying on the ground, soiled by the dirt. He is surrounded by a grassy, flowing plain. Confused, he sits up and looks down at himself. He is still in his suit and tie. Both ray guns are still in their holsters.

Was that real? Is this real?

"Hello! Anybody?" Bragg asks the air.

There is no answer.

Bragg climbs to his feet. In the distance, across a grand bridge, looms a castle-looking structure. There is nothing else but lush green plains as far as the eye can see. With no other option, Bragg starts walking toward the bridge.

Dawn slowly begins to stir. She comes to and sees that she is sitting at the bar of The Office. She is wearing a lacy stage outfit and heels. The club is empty.

I can't be here.

She gets off the bar stool and starts toward the door. She does not make it far because a heavy chain is padlocked around her ankle. It is connected to the bottom of the barstool, snagging Dawn to a halt. She begins to panic.

There is a childlike giggle from somewhere nearby, but no one appears.

"Hello?" Dawn calls, very cautiously.

A little girl trots out from the dressing room. She appears to be around seven or eight years old. Her eyes are bright and her purple hair is cut into a bob. She is dressed in pink overalls and rain boots.

"Hey, small one. Who are you?" Dawn asks.

"Who are *you?*" the girl asks.

"Listen. This is no place for a child," Dawn continues.

"Then why are *you* here?"

"I am not a child," Dawn replies. "And I don't know why I'm here. I was almost to Europa."

"Why would you go to Europa?" the little girl asks, plopping down on a bar stool.

"To escape," Dawn says.

"What are you trying to escape?"

"A bad life."

"Why is your life so bad?"

"Look! I don't mean to be rude, but who are you?"

The little girl frowns. She jumps up from the stool and starts to stomp away. Dawn realizes her only clue is fleeing.

"Wait! I'm sorry. What if . . . what if we play a game?" Dawn calls.

The offer stops the girl in her tracks. "What kind of game?"

"It's called . . . it's called The Question Game. You ask one, then me, and so on. The only rule is that the other person must answer truthfully, no matter what."

The child is reeled back in and returns to her seat.

"Great!" Dawn says. "I've already answered some of your questions, so I guess it's my turn. What is your name?"

"Dawn," the girl replies.

"Remember, you have to answer truthfully."

"I am! I wouldn't cheat! My name is Dawn," the girl insists.

"Okay," Dawn gives up. Her question only spurs more confusion about the situation.

"My turn! What is your name?" young Dawn asks.

"It's Dawn."

"We have the same name! That's nifty," the girl says, giggling.

"Okay, Dawn. My next question is, where are we? This place was destroyed back on Earth."

"I don't know where we are," young Dawn replies.

"What do you mean? How did you get here?" older Dawn presses.

"That's two questions. No cheating," the girl says. "It's my turn. What do you hope to find on Europa?"

The question catches Dawn off guard. This entire time, from the moment she learned of Europa's existence, she thought she knew why she needed to get there. But now, with the query out in the open, Dawn second guesses herself. "I want peace. A normal life."

"I thought you said we had to be honest," young Dawn says.

"I *am* being honest!" older Dawn shouts, taking the same defensive posture that her new young friend had earlier.

"You seem fun! Exciting, like me. Peace sounds boring," the girl says.

She doesn't know what she is talking about.

"It's my turn," older Dawn says sharply. "How old are you and where are your parents?"

Young Dawn laughs. "That's two questions! I'm seven and a half! That's the answer and now it's my turn again. What is so bad about your life?"

"I'm in constant danger," older Dawn says. "One crisis after another. Life in a space gang is miserable."

"You sound so cool! I'd love to be in a space gang," young Dawn says.

"No, you wouldn't. Aspire towards a profession. A career that is respectable. I dropped out of secondary school during eleventh year," older Dawn explains. "Life in a space gang will . . . it will be hard for you. As you grow into a woman, people will expect you to turn . . . I mean do uncomfortable things with your body. You will have to work harder than others to gain respect."

"Did you gain respect?" young Dawn asks.

Dawn considers how far she has come. She reflects on The Villains, on the war and aftermath. She thinks of how much she enjoys her position in the gang. "That's two questions, little one."

At the end of the path lies an enormous drawbridge. It creaks as it lowers, allowing Bragg passage along its wooden planks. The castle on the other side stretches upward past the clouds. The outside is ominous, decorated with stone gargoyles of various shapes. The stained-glass windows have iron bars across them. The entrance is an iron door, two stories high.

As Bragg approaches, the door opens by itself. It is dark inside, making it impossible to see within. Bragg starts back toward the drawbridge, but it rises again and cuts off his path.

He turns and ventures through the castle door. There are no rooms; just one grand empty space. In the middle is a spiral staircase leading all the way to the top.

Bragg ascends the stairs. Halfway up, the stained-glass windows surrounding him phase into videos. Once he stops and examines each one, he notices they are displaying memories from his life.

Being bullied in secondary school. His mother's disappointed face when he told her he had dropped out of school. The day he met Trenton. Being promoted to Squad Commander. Meeting MINERVA. Meeting Dawn.

At the top of the stairs, everything is pitch black except for a light in the distance. Cautiously Bragg starts toward the light, venturing through the darkness for what feels like forever. The area is disorienting. There seems to be nothing above or below him, as if he is walking through space.

The closer he gets to the light, the more he can make out. A cone-shaped beam illuminates a pyramid of stairs from above. The stairs appear to lead up to a throne.

Upon the throne is a giant, sitting with his hands on his knees. He is dark-skinned and muscular, despite appearing elderly. His face has at least seven decades of wrinkles. His grey hairline has receded. He is shirtless. A silky black cape is draped over his shoulders and tied around his neck.

The stairs seem to float on air, looming over Bragg once he is close. The giant stands up from his throne, towering to eight or so feet tall. He does not speak. He only stares down at Bragg with solid white eyes.

"Where am I?" Bragg asks the man.

"You come here, yet you do not know where it is?" the giant replies. His voice is celestial. It echoes.

"Is this Europa? I was aboard a ship, just entering Europa's orbit. Then . . ."

"Why are you going to Europa?" the voice interrupts from above.

"I have a group with me, seeking refuge. I've heard Europa is home to peaceful, enlightened beings," Bragg replies.

"Why are you aboard a ship meant for war, yet looking for refuge? Are *you* 'peaceful, enlightened beings'?"

The question strikes Bragg. It's hostile. It's valid.

Why should the beings on Europa accept us?

"We are not enlightened. And in the past, we have not been peaceful. However, we seek peace now," he pleads.

"Samuel," the giant says, now in a softer tone, "it is not so simple. How many people have you killed? How many people have died following you?"

How does he know my . . .

"No. I've just . . . I'm not a bad person. I've just . . ." Bragg falls to his knees. He starts to sob.

He is right. What made me believe I deserved to live on Europa?

The giant walks down from the throne. The ground shakes every time his foot touches down.

Bragg starts to draw his ray guns from beneath his jacket, but his gut tells him there is no need. The giant reaches down and places one of his enormous hands gently on Bragg's back.

"You and your crew are still aboard your ship. We are in your mind. You are not on Europa. No humans are. By your very nature, it is nearly impossible to obtain enlightenment during one of your lifetimes.

"We are beyond your comprehension. We see the universe as it really is. Eventually, you and your crew will arrive here. That time is not now."

"What do I do now?" Bragg asks.

"Are you still lonely, Samuel? Are you still being pursued? Have you not already found the paradise you seek?" the giant asks.

Bragg looks up, ruminating on what the figure has asked him. He thinks of Dawn and The Villains. He considers how long it has been since he felt alone. So much time has passed, he has forgotten what it felt like.

"I have let down those who followed me." Bragg rises to his feet.

"Something tells me they will understand," the giant says.

"We cannot go back to where we've come."

"Then don't. There are planets throughout the many star systems," the giant says.

"Our ship cannot travel that far."

"We have used our ways to modify your ship. *The Spectator* can now go wherever its crew desires. It was built to destroy; however, it has been used to protect." The giant stares into Bragg's soul. "And it will continue to do so. Do you understand?"

"You seem so familiar," Bragg says to the giant. "Have we met before?"

"We have never met. However, you know me well. Good luck."

28. The Many Star Systems
"You know The Villains are always up for an adventure."

Bragg blinks and finds himself back aboard *The Spectator*, in the pilot's seat.

Dawn is sitting in his lap, as she was before. Her face is blank.

Behind him all the other Villains are exactly as they were on the bridge, with similar expressions.

Bragg reaches around Dawn and grasps the ship's controls. He pilots *The Spectator* away from Europa's orbit.

The other Villains begin to break out of their trance.

"We are heading back toward the warp gate?" Jasmine asks from the navigator's chair.

"Europa . . . Europa is not an option," Bragg confesses.

"I saw some guy that looked like my father. He told me that it wasn't time for me to see Europa," Jasmine says.

"Some creepy little boy told me the same," Kora admits. "I thought it was a dream."

Bragg knows it was not a dream. The beings on Europa were in *their heads*. And they don't want company.

"What did you see?" Dawn whispers to Bragg.

"A man. A giant," Bragg responds. "What did you see?"

"A little girl. She seemed so familiar, but I don't think I've seen her before."

"I felt the same about the giant I saw. It felt like he was . . . me. But different."

Then it strikes Bragg. *Enlightened beings.* What if they saw enlightened versions of themselves? What if the beings *were* enlightened versions of themselves?

"I get what you mean," Dawn replies. "The little girl's name was Dawn. We talked and she helped me realize a lot."

Bragg decides not to share his thoughts with the others. As the old giant said, there is no need to explain the situation to the crew. His idea is just a theory and it doesn't change the conclusion. The Villains cannot go to Europa.

Dawn remains on Bragg's lap, holding him.

Once *The Spectator* is through the warp gate, Bragg halts the ship. He orders the crew to rest, even though he knows they won't.

Who could rest after an experience like this?

Bragg gathers the crew on the hangar deck the following morning. He sits on the nose of the Mark IX, with a view above all twenty Villains.

Each stares up at him, waiting.

"I owe you all an apology. Europa was not the solution I believed it to be," Bragg says, slightly choked up.

There is a silent pause from the crowd. Then Dawn shouts up, "You did everything you said you would do!"

The other Villains voice their agreement.

"I will ensure you all get back to Earth," Bragg says.

"What are you going to do?" Kora asks.

Bragg taps his WristTop and presses a few buttons. A map appears above the deck in holographic form, showing the entire solar system. Bragg expands the map to the surrounding space, all darkened. He presses a few more buttons and stars flicker to life, showing new solar systems.

"Bragg . . . how? " Dawn stutters.

"During my vision, the being told me The Spectator can now go wherever we want. This new information was in the system after we left Europa's orbit," Bragg says. "I guess it is a gift. MINERVA has scanned the most viable options. There are thousands."

"ALSO, THE SHIP'S ENGINES NOW APPEAR TO BE POWERED BY SOME KIND OF PERPETUAL ENERGY. THERE IS NO LONGER A NEED TO CHARGE THEM. I CANNOT EXPLAIN IT. I AM STILL ANALYZING THE TECHNOLOGY."

Kora speaks up again. "I don't want to go back to Earth. I want to see these new planets."

Mathis agrees, followed by most of the crew.

"So you all want to go gallivanting across the stars, with engines so mysterious even MINERVA doesn't know how they operate?" Jasmine asks.

Dawn smiles from ear to ear and looks to Bragg. "You know The Villains are always up for an adventure."

Bragg smiles back. "I look forward to it."

The End
The Art of Villainy
SanTaro DeBose

Thank you for reading. If you enjoyed The Art of Villainy, please consider leaving a review on its Amazon.com webpage.

For more information about the author, please visit SanTaro DeBose's author page on Amazon.com.